AT WIT'S END

A parent's guide to ending the struggle, tears, and turmoil of learning disabilities

BY • JILL STOWELL •

ACKNOWLEDGEMENTS

It is with great love, respect, and gratitude that I want to thank the following wonderful people for their teaching, guidance, and support:

Dr. Joan Smith, my dear friend and mentor, who has so graciously shared with me the incredible depth of her knowledge about the brain, learning, attention, and memory; and who sees only possibilities when it comes to people and learning.

Gayle Moyers, who shared with me her friendship and giftedness in the field of auditory processing and sound therapy, forever changing my perspective and the lives of countless children and adults.

Svea Gold, who opened my eyes to neurodevelopmental delay, and *Dr. Samuel Berne* who helped me understand and organize neurodevelopmental, motor, and visual skills training. These two giving individuals have helped us change daunting challenges into abilities.

To my students: always my teachers.

To my incredible long-time staff, *Lorena Ghale, Laura Haro, Elena Lopez, Veronica Resendiz, and Liz Sahagun,* who have been instrumental in refining our clinical techniques and making the stories in this book possible.

To my husband, David, who has continuously supported and walked alongside me in this work with
excitement, encouragement, and love.

Thank you also to the many, many professionals,
whose teaching, insight, and vision have guided my
thinking over the years, including:

Daniel Amen	*Brenda Lana*
William Bescoby	*Pat Lindamood*
Nanci Bell	*Phylis Lindamood*
Frank Belgau	*Karyn Lutes*
Jan Chamberlain	*Paul Madaule*
Alex Dolman	*Ron Minson*
Ron Davis	*Seth Mittleman*
Gail Dennison	*Marla Omar*
Paul Dennison	*Joel Roberts*
Terri Freyermuth	*Sara Rousseve*
Sheila Frick	*Pierre Sollier*
Ken Gibson	*Lena Rasmussen*
Carla Hannaford	*Thorkild Rasmussen*

Roger Stark

Deborah Sunbeck

Albert A. Sutton

Ingo Steinbach

Doug Stephey

Deborah Swain

Steve Truch

Carol Utay

Joe Utay

CONTENTS

———————————●———————————

A Note to Parents

Dear Parents...

I remember walking my five-year-old daughter to school on her first day of Kindergarten. I stood at the doorway to the classroom with the other moms and dads. We all had lumps in our throats and dreams in our hearts. This was a very big step at the beginning of that long road called "school," that would help determine our children's future.

Unfortunately, for at least three out of every ten children, the excitement of learning and dreams of success will begin to fade. They will be replaced with pain and frustration somewhere along the road. Because in spite of good intelligence, these children have some difficulty with learning.

They may have a problem learning to read or spell. Maybe they have difficulty remembering what they see or hear. Listening and paying attention may be hard. Perhaps they struggle to comprehend or to express their ideas.

Parents begin to spend hours and hours every day helping their child struggle through homework. Kids start to feel stupid and frustrated and angry. Family tension and worry rise to the breaking point because the child is taking up all of one parent's time, while the other parent and siblings feel neglected.

Learning is the most important thing we do. Not just in school but in absolutely every arena in our lives. Learning problems can affect how we see the world, how we perform at school and work, and our success in relationships. They often limit our options.

But it doesn't have to be this way. Children and adults with learning problems do not have to go through life limited or crippled by them. Learning problems, including diagnosed learning disabilities and dyslexia, can be permanently corrected so that these high potential individuals can have the opportunities and future they deserve.

I feel great urgency to get this message out to parents of children with learning challenges. If the problems are not corrected, children will suffer needlessly. They will often take a lesser path for their future because they don't have the skills or confidence to really pursue their dreams. This lesser path may mean not going to college, moving from job to job, or even a life of crime.

Frankie is a perfect example. I was a Resource Specialist (special education teacher) in public school when twelve-year-old Frankie slunk through my door. Frankie had a reputation of being a tough kid, a *really* tough kid. Even the teachers knew not to mess with Frankie. He was already entrenched in a street gang and had the belligerent attitude to go with it. Frankie was a smart kid going nowhere fast.

I owe a lot to Frankie, first and foremost an apology. I really liked him. And I felt for him. I could see how intelligent he was and how absolutely impossible reading and writing were for him. But I failed him. Like so many teachers, I really cared and I did my best, but at the end of the day, Frankie still couldn't read. And I didn't know how to teach him. I didn't know how to get to the root of the problem. I didn't even know there was a "root."

I also owe Frankie my thanks. He didn't believe he could learn, but somehow, I knew that couldn't be right. I began to search for the answers and started on the journey that has led us here today.

In this book, I want to help you, the parent, find answers.

- Why does your smart child struggle so much?
- Why doesn't anything you've tried seem to be working?
- Could there be something underlying the poor grades that is the real issue?
- If so, what is it? Can it be fixed?
- Is it really possible to correct dyslexia, learning disabilities, or other learning and attention challenges?
- *How* can these issues be corrected?
- Where do you go for help?

There *are* real solutions.

For decades, pioneers in the field of learning, many of whom are listed in the acknowledgements, have been exploring the causes and solutions for learning challenges. Today, the brain research has caught up with the clinicians. We know now that the brain can change. Learning can improve. Those dreams for your child's future can be re-captured. I hope that's what you'll take away from this book: the joy of understanding and hope, and a blueprint for real solutions.

The parent of one of our students recently wrote me this e-mail:

"You need to know, your services have been absolutely invaluable. You have given my daughter a chance to have a happy, productive life instead of one full of disappointments and frustration. Our family is functioning much more calmly as well. For that there are no words to fully express my thanks to you. Thanks for helping. Thanks for caring."

This is your story.

If your child is struggling in school, I believe you will find him or her in these pages. You will recognize yourself and your story. You'll see that you're not alone and you'll find answers. Parents, this is for you. Enjoy!

Jill Stowell, M.S., April 2010

———————————————— ● ————————————

There are 3 ideas that I want to share with you before you begin reading. These will help you put the book into perspective and act as a sort of preliminary foundation to what comes next.

First, this book is written from my point of view, based on my experiences over the last three decades working with students with learning challenges both as a public school teacher and a private practice specialist. The stories are all true. The success that our four thousand-plus students have had is real.

So exactly what is my role in all this?

Experts come in many forms. Researchers gather together two groups of students, try a technique on one group, and withhold that technique or program from the other group. In a really good research study, neither the students nor the instructor will know which group they are in.

I am not a researcher. People who come to our center do not want to sacrifice money or time in order to possibly have the best techniques withheld from their child. They come because they want results.

Evaluators (psychologists, psychiatrists, neurologists, pediatricians, testing centers) assess students on a battery of tests to find out if there is a problem and often to give it a label. I am not primarily an evaluator. Parents do not bring their children to us for me to tell them that there is some kind of problem. They already know that. What they want is a different result. That's what we do.

We are "interventionists." Our job is to use assessment results, research findings, and the most effective clinical techniques and programs available to move a student from the abilities that he has to the abilities that will change how he performs in school, in social situations, and in life.

Assessment and research are very valuable. We use information from assessment and research in what we do.

But our job is to take everything we know, take into account what the assessment results show, consider the research we have available to us, mix in experience and intuition, and then practice the art of good teaching.

In some cases, we have made discoveries before all the research has been published. Sometimes we take new research and apply it to what we have to offer students.

The bottom line is that our job is to make changes in what students can do. Much of what we have developed over the years has come when everything we knew how to do simply wasn't working...we weren't getting the changes the student needed. So we would go on a quest to find new ways of fixing learning skills.

Again, all the stories in the book are true. They happened to real students in our clinic. There will be "experts" that refute what we have done. That's OK. Sometimes, what we do flies in the face of traditional approaches and conventional wisdom.

This book is about our experiences in making learning skills work for students over the last 25 years. It has been a thrilling journey that I hope you can benefit from.

Second, this work has been focused on the population of students that fit under the umbrella of "learning disabilities." By definition, that means the student has at least average, but in many cases above average intelligence. The techniques in this book make tremendous changes in those students' abilities.

Having said that, the programs and techniques we use also make changes for other populations. They will not make a child with true mental retardation have average intelligence and they won't generally move an autistic child off the autistic spectrum. But they can greatly increase the functioning, abilities, and quality of life for these students.

Third, I know that what I write here does not fit the popular message about learning disabilities. Even some of the biggest, most powerful organizations who are experts in my field may dispute what I teach. They will tell people that learning disabilities and dyslexia are permanent conditions.

Change happens slowly in this world. Because we have seen the changes students can make, and have done it for such a long time with so many children and adults, I'm confident that at some time in the future, what I write about here will become common knowledge.

Until then, I invite you to read ahead and then go find help for your child. The answers *are* out there.

---•---

PART ONE

Navigating and Understanding the World of Dyslexia, Learning Disabilities, and Other Learning and Attention Challenges

From talking with thousands of parents over the years, I know that when your child has learning or attention problems, you feel confused and alone. Is it your fault? Is it your child's fault? Is it the teacher? Should you be doing something different? What will relatives and friends say if they know your child can't keep up?

Then one day, your smart, beautiful child comes home saying, "I'm the dumbest kid in the class," and you know you have to do something. If you can find someone who will really listen, they don't seem to get it; they don't really hear you. You get confusing messages, and almost everywhere you turn, you're told that your child will just have to live with it. There are no real solutions. You'd better change your dreams. The future will have to look different for *your* child.

Your child is misunderstood, often misdiagnosed, and left to cope. For all of you parents who have been there and think this is unacceptable, this book is for you.

In Part One, we will explore your journey, what's true and what's not about learning challenges and what the underlying roots of the learning, behavior, social, and attention challenges are.

There *are* real and permanent solutions. Your child can achieve the future you know he or she has the potential to have. Part One will help you understand why.

————————————————— ● —————————————————

The Faces of Learning Problems

Is your child one of the 14.9 million children in America struggling with reading or school? Who are these children? What do they look like?

In this chapter. . .
- Why a learning problem may be dismissed altogether or attributed to the wrong cause.
- Without proper treatment, learning disabilities typically last a lifetime and are not something children simply outgrow.
- Many children with learning difficulties are very bright.
- Children with learning disabilities are usually doing the best they can, but won't reach their full potential without help.

Chatting with friends and making jokes gets Mike through his day at school. Of course, his teacher is extremely irritated with him for constantly disrupting the class with his talking and his jokes. And she cannot understand how such a smart boy can refuse to do his work and get so little accomplished during the day.

The truth about Mike is that he *is* very intelligent, but he can't read very well. His intelligence gets him by; he can read enough to sometimes get answers right, to sometimes get parts of assignments completed. Unfortunately, he can get just enough done to make it look like he can do it, so when he doesn't, he looks unmotivated.

Mike's teacher thinks he has Attention Deficit Disorder. In reality, Mike is dyslexic. He can't do the work, so he finds other ways to entertain himself. He's getting Fs in 4th grade. Mike's mother sees how hard he tries at home, but even she is frustrated because Mike can't seem to get any of his homework done without her there helping every minute. Dad is mad because he thinks Mike could do better if he tried harder. And Mike just wants to give up. No matter how hard he tries, he still can't manage to make the grade.

A concussion can trigger learning problems.

Soccer is what Mindy lives for. She's one of the best on her team, and she plans to go to college on a soccer scholarship. That is, if she can get her grades up. Ever since starting high school, Mindy has been struggling more than usual to get good grades in class. In fact, she's only pulling Ds in some classes now.

School has always been hard for Mindy, but she's a worker. She's motivated. So she has sweated blood over the years and gotten pretty good grades, grades that probably would have been good enough when paired with her outstanding ability in soccer.

But shortly before beginning high school, Mindy got a concussion playing soccer. Ever since, her thinking has been more disorganized. She still tries really hard, but somehow, she just can't seem to remember things as well as she used to. She forgets where she put assignments and often doesn't quite understand what the teacher is saying in class. She misunderstands directions and sometimes even gets confused in conversations with her friends. All of this, on top of the reading problems that she worked so hard to compensate for over the years, is making school almost impossible.

Non-stop chatter and lack of focus isolates a child.

Speed is the name of the game for Eddie, an extremely bright, energetic 5th grade boy with boundless energy. Eddie has so much to say that he just knows everyone wants to hear—right now! He's the first one done in class, and his work is usually right. He explodes out to recess the second the bell rings and pesters everyone on the playground with his non-stop chatter and his enthusiastic grabbing at classmates to get them to come along and play.

When recess is over, Eddie can't begin to pull all that energy back in to focus again for another two hours, so he's chattering and popping in and out of his seat constantly. Instead of raising his hand to speak, he blurts out the answers before anyone else has a chance. He speaks very loudly, and though he is a boy with great intentions and a heart of gold, he has no friends and is driving his teachers crazy.

"Pay attention, Eddie!" has become a mantra in his classes, but try as he might, he just cannot seem to contain his words and keep his body in the chair. His classmates are constantly shushing him, which makes him feel angry. Eddie so desires to have friends and is hurt and confused because no one seems to want to be around him.

When children can't keep up, they assume they're stupid.

Regular kids, with average to above average intelligence are sitting in class, day after day, frustrated and misunderstood by their teachers, parents, classmates, and even themselves. They want to do well in school. They know they should be able to. But somehow, they just can't seem to do it.

Why does it take them so long to finish their work? Why is Johnny, sitting next to them, already finished while they're only on problem number two? Why do they have hours more homework than other kids in their class? Are they just stupid? "Must be," they conclude, "since everyone else seems to be able to do the work more easily."

Surprisingly, these kids exist in every classroom in every school. They might be good at hiding it, but they are suffering nevertheless. Somehow, no matter how good they are at other things, reading or math or some other aspect of school just isn't working out for them as well as it should.

Learning problems can be caused by a variety of factors, but by far, the most common reason for a child to struggle in school is weak learning skills or what you might think of as information processing skills. In her research in the 1970s, Patricia Lindamood found that approximately 30 percent of people across all populations—socio-economic, geographic, ethnic, and age—have some degree of difficulty with processing the sounds in words. This is a critical factor in learning to read and spell. As a result of this factor alone, at least 3 out of 10 children in every classroom and 3 out of 10 adults are less efficient than they could be with reading.

School is a child's job. When learning is difficult, there will almost always be a cost in time, energy, and emotion. If the challenges go uncorrected, the cost may go well beyond grades to affect a child's relationships, self-esteem, and choices.

Struggling to find a place to excel

I recently spoke to a parent who shared that she was at her wit's end over her fourteen-year-old son. He had a history of not doing well in school. He was smart enough and never qualified for any kind of special help at school, but somehow, he didn't seem to understand what was going on in class or what he was supposed to do on assignments . . . so he quit doing them and found other ways to occupy his time. At the time I spoke to his mother, he had just gotten arrested for shoplifting. When asked why he did it, he replied, "At least it's something I'm good at." To my knowledge, this boy never got help for his learning problems. It breaks my heart to think what his future may be like.

How the brain processes information
dramatically affects learning.

Michael's story has a similar beginning. Michael was in 8th grade when I met him. He had few friends, and he was literally failing in school. On top of that, he was so anxious about his poor performance in school that he had severe migraines and stomachaches three to four times a week.

Testing revealed that Michael had a serious auditory processing problem. His hearing was normal; his ears could hear, but the messages getting to the brain were not always clear and complete. Listening for Michael was like having a bad cell phone connection *all the time.*

No wonder Michael could not follow directions that were told to him. No wonder he was confused in class and couldn't connect well in conversations. He was getting spotty, partial information. He tried hard to understand, but was missing so much important information that he felt lost all of the time. He was a high achiever at heart, so this caused a tremendous amount of anxiety.

All of this changed for Michael when he began working on improving his listening skills through a specialized *Auditory Stimulation and Training* program at our learning center. Within a few weeks, his headaches and stomachaches began to disappear. By the end of the semester, Michael had made friends and was on the honor roll.

A few years later, I ran into Michael, and he very proudly reported that he was a straight-A student and the ASB president of his high school. Recently, Michael called to tell me that he was one of sixty students in the country who had received early acceptance into the prestigious Brown Medical School.

These two similar boys with similar learning challenges headed down very different paths. Michael shared that the turning point for him was when he started his specialized program of auditory stimulation and training that retrained his brain to listen.

Why children can be excellent in one area and weak in another

Learning disabilities have sometimes been referred to as the "invisible disability." Often, children with serious learning challenges at school exhibit strong abilities and talents in other areas. I have witnessed the creation of incredible Lego structures in my waiting room from children who stammer and stumble over simple reading passages. Recently, I met a young man who is brilliant in physics and chemistry, but who takes hours to read a chapter in his history book. Children who cannot spell or write a good paragraph are sometimes wonderful storytellers.

Children with learning disabilities often have what seem like extreme strengths and weaknesses. They may excel in sports or in artistic, creative, or mechanical arenas. They may be the one the family turns to when something is broken, because somehow, they can just "see" how to fix it. One of our most challenged learners when it comes to attention, reading, writing, and math, has already planned out the intricate details of an invention that he's going to create for his school science fair.

This is one of the confusing things about children with learning challenges. How can they be so talented in one area but do so poorly in others? It is encouraging to know that many actors, inventors, business leaders, and sports celebrities had dyslexia or other learning disabilities and "made it." But it's also important to keep in mind that only a very few people actually win the Olympics, build Fortune 500 companies, or invent something life-changing like the light bulb. We need to celebrate the accomplishments and strengths of our children, but we cannot assume that a child's talents will override his challenges if he struggles with learning.

I once had a dad say of his eleven-year-old son, "He doesn't need to read well. He's going to be a professional ball player." I sincerely hope that was true, but at eleven years old, do we really want to count on that?

Growing up doesn't mean growing out of learning challenges.

Getting out of high school can sometimes be a relief to students with learning challenges, but just because they grow up doesn't mean that the learning challenges go away. Those who go on to college often find that in spite of their determination, they have to work much harder and longer than their peers, and it's hard to stick with it.

Bright men and women who were frustrated and challenged as children in school often find themselves in unfulfilling jobs, unemployment lines, or worse yet, in jail. Underachievement and frustration in school because of learning challenges, unfortunately, often leads to underachievement and frustration in life and relationships outside of school as well.

John was a stuntman in the movies. He had graduated from high school unable to read and was still a non-reader at twenty-six when I met him. As successful as he was in the movie industry, he wasn't where he wanted to be because of his reading disability. He shared that he didn't want to "beat-up his body" being a stuntman for the rest of his life; he wanted to act. But, of course, he couldn't go to auditions where he had to read, and he lived in fear that someone might find out and he'd be kicked off the set as a danger because he couldn't read the signs.

John had a job, but it wasn't the one he wanted, and the embarrassment and frustration he had lived with through school, followed him into his adult life. Eventually, that frustration led John to get the kind of help that could solve his dyslexia and open the door for the acting career he desired.

What does it feel like to live with a learning challenge?

What does it mean if you're the child in the neighborhood that has a learning challenge? For twelve-year-old Jenny, it means you feel stupid because you study all the time and you get Ds and Fs on most of your papers anyway. For nine-year-old Robbie, it means that you're angry and ready to fight all the time because kids on the playground make fun of you for going to a special class.

Andy is worried that he won't get to play sports next semester in high school because he can't keep his grades up. He lives for sports and doesn't know how he's going to take it if he can't do the one thing he really feels good at.

Kailee is in 2nd grade and has already figured out that if she's really helpful and really nice, she can sometimes get out of doing her work in class. When she takes it home, her mom sits with her and helps her get it all done right. So far, no one at school knows Kailee's secret. But Kailee knows she can't do the work the way everyone else can, and she has stomachaches everyday.

Josh is the class clown. Sure, he gets in trouble a lot for disrupting the class, but he's really funny. Even the teacher laughs sometimes and the kids really like him. As long as he can talk and entertain people, nobody seems to realize that he can't do the work.

Most students with learning challenges have at least average to above average intelligence. They're capable kids who know they should be doing better. They deal with it in different ways, but the bottom line is that having difficulty learning is painful, embarrassing, and confusing. It affects how they feel about themselves, the choices they make, their relationships, and their future.

Families are affected by learning challenges as well. Often, the child who is struggling needs so much help and attention that other children in the family feel neglected. Battles over homework take their toll on time and energy for other activities. And for parents, it is heartbreaking to watch their child struggle and not know how to fix it.

Learning challenges can affect more than schoolwork.

Sometimes, learning problems are almost exclusively related to schoolwork or reading, but many times, the underlying challenges causing the problems in school carry over into life in general. Do you see your child in any of these examples?

- Andy never knows where he's supposed to be on the soccer field.
- Kenny always seems to swing too early in baseball practice.
- Rachel walks on her toes.
- Sam is nine and still doesn't know how to ride a bike.
- Sally seems to be in a world of her own, always happy, but always drifting around with no real sense of direction.
- Cal hates change and gets really upset when anything in the family schedule changes.
- Kara keeps failing her driving test because she can't parallel park.
- Mandy is bossy and demands her own way or she doesn't want to play.
- Danny talks non-stop and monopolizes every conversation at Boy Scouts and in his church youth group.
- Aiden can't carry on a conversation on the phone.
- Alan's moods are up and down. He's smart and talented but "down" most of the time.
- Cindy is awkward and doesn't understand social space so she makes people uncomfortable.
- David is going in 4th grade, but he still gets anxious whenever he goes somewhere without a parent.

- Nick does everything his friends tell him to do because he's too timid to say no.
- Alexis has never been to a birthday party because she doesn't have any friends.

Correct diagnosis and treatment changes lives.

Life is all about learning. The root causes of academic struggles show up in other areas of a child's life. These things may baffle and confuse parents, but are often passed off as personality traits, quirks, or preferences.

One of the things we love about fixing underlying learning skills is that not only do school learning problems get resolved, but other aspects of life seem to become easier and more fluid as well. Parents often comment that their child seems "more confident and mature." Maturity is more than just a matter of time. It occurs as children gain more awareness, internal organization, and control.

Friendships are one of the most heartwarming outcomes of improved underlying learning skills. One of our nineteen-year-old clients who had always had trouble making friends, shared after four weeks of sound therapy that he had gone out that weekend and met some new people and actually talked to them. He said, "They treated me like a *leader* and acted like they really *liked* me!" So often, the underlying challenges that affect academic progress also get in the way of social relationships.

It is with great respect and passion that I write this book about solving learning challenges. The students mentioned are real, though names have been changed. These are amazing individuals of all ages, who are smart, motivated, and every bit as deserving of a promising future as every other child in their school. They may look lazy. They may look like underachievers. They may have developed irritating coping strategies.

But these students want desperately to succeed and are working with so much more effort and energy than anyone would guess. They plug away for years through the discouragement of poor performance. They should be applauded, and they should be helped.

Throughout this book, I will refer to "children." I intend this to include teens, but the learning challenges and solutions presented here are not exclusive to children and teens. They are just as applicable to the millions of adults with dyslexia, ADHD, and other learning challenges.

Parents hate seeing their children struggling or in pain. When a child has difficulty learning, parents often don't know where to turn. Or they are immobilized by too many opinions and conflicting messages. My goal in this book is to help you, the parent, gain a better understanding of the problem, and most importantly, the solutions. Yes! These are real solutions that remove barriers to learning and truly open the way to a brighter future.

Action items. . .

- Read this book with sticky notes or a highlighter in hand to mark the sections that apply to your child.
- Change your mindset from frustration to hope because proper diagnosis and drug-free treatment can solve the underlying problems causing most learning challenges.
- Go to www.LearningDisability.com.
  Under "Free Articles," read:
  - * "7 Things Every Parent Should Know about Learning Challenges."
- Go to www.FixLearningSkills.com.
  - * Listen to "The Many Faces of Learning Problems."
  - * Watch the video, "What if. . ."

CHAPTER 2

7 Myths and the Truth about Learning Problems

*Find out how common beliefs about learning problems
are crippling children and adults who have them.*

In this chapter. . .

- Seven common myths that haunt children with learning disabilities
- Why it's so confusing for both parents and children to reconcile poor performance in smart children
- The revolutionary truth that many experts completely deny

**Overcoming learning disabilities paves the way
for a child to reach his full potential.**

Bright-eyed, nine-year-old Darren walked into my office with a bounce in his step. He was such a "together" kid, conversing easily with me, polite to his mom, interesting and interested in everything. You would never know it by looking at him or talking to him, but Darren couldn't read. Not a word!

Darren's reading goal for the year in his special education class was: "Darren will read ten survival words." Ten words in a whole year? Nobody believed this boy would ever read! But Darren's mom would not settle for her intelligent, gregarious, verbal child being a non-reader for life. She could not buy into the myth that once dyslexic always dyslexic.

Darren and his mom worked with us at the learning center in specialized programs to solve the underlying issues causing his confusion with sounds and letters. By the time he was in junior high school, he was no longer in special education, and no one believed that he had ever had a reading problem. Darren took Advanced Placement classes in high school and graduated with honors. When I last saw him, he was a happy, confident theater major in college. That's a long way from learning ten survival words in a year of school.

Many children don't get the chance that Darren did, because many parents and teachers don't know that the myths about learning problems simply aren't true.

Myth #1: People with learning challenges just aren't that smart.

Joe drags himself to school everyday, wishing he could hide under a rock. It's so embarrassing when he gets called on to read in class and his classmates or teacher have to help him with most of the words. He tries desperately to use the words he knows to help him figure out the ones he doesn't, but it takes so much time. If only there were more pictures in the 6th grade text. Then he could piece together the story and sound like he knew what he was doing. Ha! Maybe he's just stupid. That's what the class bully says out loud and what all the other kids are probably saying to themselves.

Many people believe that students who struggle with reading or other aspects of school just aren't that smart. Take Joe, for example. He didn't begin learning to read until he was twelve.

But let's fast-forward nine years. By the time he was twenty-one, Joe had figured out how to play the stock market so well that he was a millionaire. When I met him twenty years later he was a multi-millionaire. That doesn't sound like a guy who wasn't that smart!

Students with learning disabilities are smart enough and often smarter than average.

By definition, students diagnosed with learning disabilities have at least average to above average intelligence. Many of the students who come through our clinic are very bright or even gifted. This is one of the things that is so confusing for parents, relatives, and teachers. They can see that the student appears bright, but certain aspects of learning at school simply elude her. It just doesn't seem to match up.

Myth #2: "These kids don't really have a problem. They're just lazy. They need to try harder."

Vince's parents were heartbroken—heartbroken and elated—when they learned that Vince had auditory processing weaknesses which were causing his problems in school. They were elated because now maybe something could be done to help him reach his potential and feel better about himself, but heartbroken because for years they had accused Vince of being lazy. They had punished him for not trying harder. Understanding the real cause of his poor performance made everything make sense.

Vince had trouble following directions. He never seemed to be sure what his homework was. He always seemed to be operating with a partial set of information. Even in conversation, he seemed a little lost. Vince "tried harder" for many years, but by the time he was in high school, he'd figured out that "trying harder" wasn't working, so he just quit trying at all.

Learning problems can be disguised as laziness.

In our twenty-five years of working with children and adults with various learning challenges, I have yet to meet a student who was truly lazy. "Lazy" is a symptom but is rarely, if ever, the real issue. When students aren't doing their work, it's most likely because they don't have a complete enough set of skills to do the job.

In Vince's case, his auditory processing delays caused him to miss just enough information that he would think he understood the lesson or assignment, but when he sat down to do the work, he was really confused. He'd sit and stare at the page, hoping it would somehow make sense to him, but eventually, he became unwilling to put out the effort.

For years, Vince's parents had helped him go over and over information for tests, but when the questions were stated differently than the way he had studied, he just couldn't make the connection. How many times are we willing to put out great amounts of effort only to fail? Surprisingly, those "lazy" looking kids with learning challenges often hang in there far longer than most people would tolerate.

Myth #3: Kids who do poorly in school just don't care. They're unmotivated.

Getting your double axel is a big deal for an ice skater. It's one of those really huge, really difficult milestones. I know this because my daughter is a figure skater. At twelve years old, she really wanted two things: to get her double axel and to have a pair of Doc Martins (shoes). I certainly wasn't inclined to buy a hundred-dollar pair of shoes for a girl whose feet were still growing.

But Christy was almost there with her double axel, so close her coach could taste it! One day, he told her he would give her a hundred dollar bill if she would land the double axel right now. Was she motivated? Absolutely! Did she land it? No. Her coach would never offer her that deal now, since she can practically do a double axel in her sleep, but at the time, she just didn't quite have the skills. If you don't have the skills to do the job, it really doesn't matter how motivated you are.

Lack of skills, not lack of motivation, is often the issue.

Imagine that every time you open a book to read the page looks like this to you:

Mha tif baqe the lookeb lik eth is when you rtied
ot reab? Wonld yon relaly wauf to read? Moulb
it make ony wanj ot try harber or jnst wnatto thorm
the dook onutthe min dow?

How motivated would you be to read? And even if you were highly motivated, how well would you do? My experience with children with learning challenges is that they care deeply. If they look unmotivated, it's a symptom, not the problem. Sometimes, it's just easier to fail on purpose than to know you tried your best and failed anyway.

Myth #4: If you aren't *diagnosed* learning disabled, dyslexic, or ADHD, then you don't have a learning problem. Nothing's wrong.

When children are struggling with reading, math, or some other aspect of learning, parents usually know. Moms know for sure. But sometimes when a parent asks for testing at school, they're told that there's nothing wrong, that their child is doing fine.

Other times, children do go through the testing but don't qualify for special education services at school.

When a child doesn't fit the diagnosis of learning disability, dyslexia, or attention deficit hyperactivity disorder, the common belief is that there is nothing wrong. The child just isn't that smart or needs to try harder. Families go back to toughing it out through hours of homework, tears, and discouragement, wondering what they might have done to cause this.

The truth is that most learning challenges are caused by a weakness in one or more areas of underlying learning skills. These are not academic skills, like reading and writing, but the brain's information processing skills. If we are going to learn, we have to be able to take in accurate and complete information through our senses, remember it, think about it, and organize it for learning. We call these "learning skills."

The "official" criteria for learning disabilities misses many children who need help.

Only about five to nine percent of school-age children are diagnosed with learning disabilities, but research tells us that *at least* 30 percent have some degree of weakness with underlying processing or learning skills. This means that 21–25 percent of the children in school will never formally qualify as learning disabled but struggle to learn nevertheless.

When a parent brings a child to our clinic, we want to know what the challenges look like in real life: at home, in school, on the playground, and doing homework. What academic areas are affected? Then we begin our search to find out what underlying learning skills are not supporting the student well enough. The challenges are real, whether formally diagnosed or not, and the underlying learning skills are the place to begin to correct them.

Myth #5: Children with learning problems just need time. They'll grow out of it.

"Don't worry, he's a boy! Give him time. He'll grow out of it." How many parents have heard these words from well-meaning teachers and relatives, only to regret not taking action sooner?

If maturity is truly the issue behind difficulties in school, then time is the answer. But retaining a child in a grade level or just waiting for her to grow up will not solve a learning disability or a learning skills problem.

Kevin was a little boy full of the boundless energy that four-and-a-half-year-olds have. He was coordinated, smart, and talkative. He was scheduled to begin kindergarten in the fall in a very academic school. He would be almost five. But Kevin had no interest in letters or numbers or worksheets in preschool. His name writing and copying were immature. Kevin's preschool teacher wisely advised his parents to give him time by putting him in pre-kindergarten in September.

For Kevin, this was a very good decision. His challenge with school was not a learning disability. He was simply young, chronologically and developmentally. Another year of maturity before hitting the academic scene was exactly what he needed.

Mark was seven when his teacher suggested that he be retained in first grade. He was friendly, talkative, charming, and coordinated. But he couldn't read. He still couldn't say the names of all the letters and when he "read" in his reading book, he simply looked at the pictures and made up a story. Mark turned letters upside down or backwards when writing and at seven years old was already "losing" his papers and coming up with clever excuses for not doing his work.

Mark had a strong dyslexic thinking style. Time and maturity were not going to change that. In fact, another year in first grade, without the right kind of intervention to solve the reading challenges would only serve to erode his confidence and make him feel like a failure. He'd be taller and older, but he'd still be way behind the others.

Left untreated, learning disabilities are life-long hindrances.

A learning skills or processing problem is not something that a child grows out of. It accompanies him and frustrates him into adulthood. Age just allows him to find better ways to get around it. Mark learned to avoid reading by asking to go to the bathroom or the nurse. His father, also dyslexic, found a more grown-up way to avoid reading. He went into his own business and hired someone to do any reading and writing that was required.

Myth #6: The best way to help someone with a learning problem is to help him get around it—to make accommodations.

Ten-year-old Jake was a smart boy with serious learning problems in the areas of auditory processing, reading, writing, and math. To help him at school, Jake was given a one-to-one instructional aide who sat with him in class. Jake couldn't understand the teacher's instructions, so his aide repeated them more slowly and simply. He couldn't do the math or reading that the rest of the students were doing, so his aide worked with him in the back of the class doing lower level work. With her at his side, Jake could get some work done. But he wasn't progressing, and the problem wasn't changing. Jake was getting through school, but he wasn't becoming independent. What would the future look like for him when his aide wasn't there?

Tony was a young adult with a reading disability. He'd figured out some very clever accommodations for himself. He'd apply for jobs with a sling on his arm so that he'd have an excuse to take the application home where someone could read it and write it for him. He'd always order last in a restaurant so that he could order the same thing as someone else. He'd press the record button on his answering machine whenever someone was giving him an address or directions that needed to be written down.

Adapting rather than solving underlying problems is a stop-gap measure.

Accommodations, such as more time on tests, having tests read to them, giving oral rather than written reports, and having fewer spelling words, are common and helpful to students struggling in school. The problem is that accommodations are not addressing the real issue; they're just helping students live with it.

Accommodating a learning problem is like riding a bike with a flat tire. With lots of extra effort and someone holding the seat, it can be done. But wouldn't it be better just to fix the flat tire? Tony was a great guy and obviously very inventive to have come up with such creative ways to get around his dyslexia, but he felt so much more confident and independent once he got help to fix the underlying learning skills that had kept him from being able to learn to read and write on his own.

Myth #7: A learning problem is a permanent condition.

Jan had always believed what her parents, teachers, and doctor believed: that her dyslexia was a permanent condition. When Jan found out that her nine-year-old daughter Leah also had learning disabilities, she refused to buy into the myth anymore. Her pain was one thing, but she was not about to watch her daughter go through what she had.

Jan got help for Leah and was relieved to see that once Leah's underlying learning skills improved, she was able to learn to read and write. When Leah made the honor roll in 4th grade, Jan was inspired to get help for herself. She went through the same kind of cognitive training and reading remediation programs that Leah had gone through. Then she went to college—something she had always wanted to do—and was thrilled to report that the first A she had ever received was in her college English class.

Good news! Leaning disabilities don't have to be permanent.

For twenty-five years, we have seen the lives of thousands of children and adults changed by permanently solving their learning challenges, including dyslexia and other learning disabilities. We now live in a remarkable world where brain research is possible. In the last twenty years, brain research has validated that the brain can change, not just during a small window of time in childhood, but anytime. With specific, intensive training, the brain can learn to think about and process information in new and more efficient ways.

To all of you parents who refused to believe the myth, you were right. A learning problem does NOT have to be a permanent condition.

Action items. . .

- Go to www.LearningDisability.com.
  Under "Free Articles" read:
  - ∗ "Not Just Laziness."
  - ∗ "Maybe He's Just Lazy!"
- Go to www.FixLearningSkills.com.
  - ∗ Listen to "3 Myths About Learning Problems."

———————————————— • ————

How Do I Know if My Child Has a Learning Problem?

Here are some red flags and symptoms
to help you determine if help is needed.

In this chapter. . .
- Parents are most likely to notice potential problems in their children.
- The distinctions that help a parent tell the difference between normal responses to schoolwork and social situations, and the symptoms of learning disabilities.
- The early signs to watch for in preschoolers.

Common signs of learning problems

Moms are very astute when it comes to their children, so when something's not right, moms usually know. Typical children feel overwhelmed or unhappy about homework at times. They may even come home saying they feel stupid or hate school once in a while. But when an otherwise happy energized child routinely whines, sobs, and wilts at the thought of homework or school, or berates himself for his stupidity, it is very likely that learning is harder than it should be.

While doing homework with their children, parents often notice things that don't seem quite right and wonder if this is typical or if what they are seeing is a sign of a problem. Here are some "red flags" that we commonly hear from parents about their children:

Reading:
- Don't recognize words that they read earlier on the page
- Have to sound out every single word when reading

- Add, change, omit, or repeat sounds in words
- Skip or change small common words like *the, of,* and *to*
- Have trouble sounding out words for reading
- Can't remember or tell about what they read

Spelling:

- Can remember words for the spelling test but can't spell them correctly the next week
- Have to spend an excessive amount of time trying to learn spelling words

Writing:

- Take forever to do writing assignments because they can't think of anything to write
- Have great ideas when speaking but can't seem to put them on paper
- Write with much simpler vocabulary than they use when speaking
- Have terrible handwriting
- Have a killer grip on the pencil
- Have extremely dark or very light wispy writing
- Have poor letter formation when writing

Speaking:

- Words or ideas get out of sequence
- Have trouble expressing themselves so they give up
- Have poor articulation
- Mumble or slur words

Math:

- Can't remember math facts
- Don't understand math concepts
- May seem like they've got it one minute and then act completely confused the next
- Make many "careless" errors

General:

- Not keeping up in school
- Poor self-esteem
- Low confidence

- Spend hours longer on homework than their classmates
- Can't do homework unless a parent is sitting right there

Dr. Ken Gibson, president of Learning Rx, says, "A person has a learning problem if (s)he makes more <u>mistakes</u> than the average person, takes <u>longer</u> than the average person, or has to <u>work harder</u> than the average person." I recently heard a parent say, "I wonder what grade I'm going to get in 5th grade this year?" It was a joke, but not really. If you feel like you're doing most of the work, your child's underlying learning skills are probably not supporting her well enough.

Watch for signs of anxiety.

Anxiety can also be a symptom of a learning problem. Parents are sometimes led to believe that there is something "psychologically" wrong with their child or their parenting, and if so, this certainly shouldn't be ignored. But poor performance at school can cause a perfectly normal child with a supportive family to experience a great deal of anxiety. Children with learning challenges live in fear of doing something stupid or having their difficulties noticed. Their internal chatter may be saying:

- What if the other kids see my bad grade?
- What if I'm the last one done?
- What if I don't know where we are when the teacher calls on me?
- What if I say something stupid and everyone laughs at me?
- What if bump into someone in line again and get into trouble?

Children display anxiety in a variety of ways.

Kara was an adorable, chatty, seven-year-old with a family history of dyslexia. She was extremely confused about letters and numbers. She couldn't write them or recognize them, but she always tried, no matter what. She became so anxious about school that she would bite her fingernails until they bled. She began to have bowel "accidents" at school.

Sal was so anxious about his poor performance in math that he became math phobic. Every time he would have to go to his math class, he would feel sick and often went to the nurse to go home. When we met him at fourteen years old, he kept his head and eyes down and literally hid behind his hair. He only grunted when spoken to, and he had been pegged as a sullen, unmotivated teenager.

Through the use of sound therapy to improve his auditory processing and a specialized math program to help math make sense, Sal came out of his shell and out from under his hair. His confidence and demeanor improved, along with his math, and he soon became a peer tutor for other students in his math class.

If I can't succeed in class, I'll . . .

Johnny's a very poor speller, but he's a really funny guy, so during spelling time, he pokes his neighbor and makes jokes to get everybody laughing.

Natalie hates seeing her dad's disappointed look when she shows him yet another math test with an F on it. So Natalie has learned to "lose" her math tests before her dad gets a chance to look at them.

Stephen gets very sleepy when reading. In fact, he hates to read. He learns best by listening. Stephen has found that if he helps girls with math, they'll tell him what the chapter in literature was about, and he never has to crack the book.

Greg gets angry and refuses to do his work. Samantha gets weepy so her mom will help her. Kyle studies late into the night and gets up early in order to get his work done. Brad brags that he's so good at sports that he doesn't have to do well in school.

People want to succeed, and when they can't, they find ways to avoid, cover, or compensate. Watching for these kinds of behaviors may help parents recognize when their children are struggling in school. If children could be successful in school, they would. It's too embarrassing and painful not to.

If my child can't pay attention in school
does it mean she has Attention Deficit Disorder?

Problems paying attention in class can be a sign to parents that their child is struggling in school. Poor listening or comprehension skills will make it difficult for a learner to follow what the teacher is saying. When enough information has been lost, attention will be lost as well. For six weeks when I was in college, I was immersed in Italian language in Italy. I recall sometimes being so tired from working so hard to listen, that I could no longer keep my attention from drifting in and out while people were talking.

Struggling readers who have to put excessive energy into figuring out the words will tend to fatigue quickly and lose attention. With little energy left for comprehension, reading may feel so hard or so boring that the student has to get distracted in order to give himself a mental break or wake himself up.

There is a very specific set of symptoms that physicians and psychologists use to determine whether or not a person has Attention Deficit Disorder. Many of these symptoms look very much like the symptoms of weak learning skills. Whenever an area of processing is inefficient, extra energy will be needed to perform. This stresses the person's attention. It is important to look very carefully to determine if the attention challenges the teacher is reporting are the cause of the learning problem or the symptom.

Can my child's social behavior be related to a learning problem?

The same learning skills that support easy, comfortable learning also provide the foundation for social skills and life outside the classroom.

Michelle withdraws and gets very quiet and in her own world in restaurants or social gatherings. Her weak listening skills make it impossible for her to keep track of conversations in a noisy room and cause her to feel lost and insecure.

Randy also has weak listening skills, but he handles it by dominating every conversation. He talks too much, too fast, and too loud. As long as he has the floor, he doesn't have to listen.

Jamie is fearful in new situations. It's hard for him to "see" the big picture of what's going on around him and to process it all fast

27

enough to feel safe and in control. He feels much more secure with the routine and familiar.

Halie has poor body awareness and control, so when she's standing in line on the playground, she often bumps into her classmates. She's always getting into trouble for not keeping her hands and feet to herself, and other children are starting to say she's mean.

Sasha comes home from school crying on a regular basis because she's had an argument with her friends, but she doesn't know why. Her poor comprehension causes her to misinterpret what other people say, leading to blame, hurt feelings, and arguments.

Parents frequently voice the concern that their child doesn't have many friends. A very encouraging outcome of improved learning skills is an improved social life.

Recognizing the invisible disability

Shawn is a really "together" thirteen-year-old. He's got a fantastic smile and a confident, friendly manner. He's an excellent soccer player and an A and B student. He aspires to be an actor and already has a few commercials under his belt. It would surprise almost anyone to know that Shawn is dyslexic. He seems to have it all in every area except this one. For Shawn, the challenges are isolated specifically to reading and spelling.

Anyone seeing Jessica walking around the halls at the high school would think she had it altogether, but her report card told a completely different story. She was getting Fs and Ds in all of her classes. Jessica was in all regular classes. She could do the work; she just couldn't manage to organize herself to get it done, get it in, or remember the information for tests. After twelve weeks of processing skills training to strengthen her underlying learning skills, Jessica's grades went up to As and Bs. In fact, she became the top student in her dreaded history class.

Just as every person is different, every student with a learning challenge is affected differently. For some students, weak underlying learning skills may cause so much disruption to learning that the challenges are very obvious, but for others, the problems may be much more subtle and harder to recognize or understand.

Grades may tell the story, but not always. In spite of good grades and strengths in and out of school, parents or students themselves may suspect that something is getting in the way of their performing as easily, efficiently, or as well as they could. Trust those instincts. You're probably right.

My child seems so immature. Could that be the problem?

It is not uncommon for a child to be six months to a year young for his chronological age. This is an important consideration when determining when a child should begin kindergarten, especially if he would also be chronologically young in his grade as well. However, appropriately mature behavior for one's age depends heavily upon a solid foundation of learning/processing skills.

How we respond to things is directly related to how we perceive them. If we are not getting accurate or complete information to think with, our responses will be less flexible and less mature. Very immature behavior is more likely a symptom of a learning problem than the cause. In fact, "maturity" is a typical outcome of improved learning skills, even in adults.

What are some early warning signs that parents might watch for in preschool children?

It is never too late to get help for a learning problem, but recognizing and correcting the challenges early can save the child and the family frustration down the road.

Jeremy's mom brought him to our learning center when he was four because he was barely talking. The root of the problem was poor auditory processing. By stimulating the auditory system early, Jeremy was able to enter kindergarten with a very appropriate vocabulary and never had to experience the reading problems that often accompany delayed speech and auditory skills.

Here are a few red flags that parents can watch out for in their preschool children. These may be early indicators of reading difficulties, particularly if there is a family history of dyslexia or other learning challenges.

- Start talking later than most children
- Difficulty with rhyming
- Difficulty pronouncing words ("busketti" for spaghetti, "dus" for bus)
- Trouble remembering nursery rhymes and prayers
- Slower to come up with the right word for the right context
- Difficulty learning numbers, days of the week, colors, shapes, and how to spell and write his name.

My experience, both as a parent and over the years working with thousands of families, is that parents know their children better than anyone else. If your instincts tell you that your child is struggling in school or you suspect that your child has a learning problem, you are probably right. This doesn't mean you should panic, but don't be afraid to investigate and see if there are things that can be done to make the education road a little easier and more enjoyable for your child.

Action items. . .
- Go to www.LearningDisability.com.
  Under "Free Articles," read:
  * "Fun, Frantic, and Fantastic: Going through the Motions with Your Four Year Old."
  * "Comfortable, Independent Learners."
  * "Helping Students Study."
- Go to www.FixLearningSkills.com.
  * Listen to "Why Does My Kid Act Like That?"

———————————————————●———

CHAPTER 4

The Parents' Journey

What do you do when you know your child is struggling in school? Find out how to sort through and understand the options.

In this chapter. . .
- The challenges parents face in trying to get answers and solutions
- The most common options parents pursue while trying to get help
- Getting to the root of the problem . . . without drugs

The agony of a parent at wit's end

I was sitting on a plane this morning when I began to write this chapter. When Allan, the man sitting next to me, found out what I did, he asked, "Do you know anything about ADHD?" He went on to share an all-too-common story.

"My son has ADHD. He's almost eighteen and never wants to do anything. He just quit high school and is doing independent study. I don't know how that will work, since he never did anything independently in school. He can do the work. He just doesn't.

He likes things like fishing and outdoor activities. I found him information about a small college that has a fishing major. He could be some kind of a guide or something. I told him I'd pay for it if he'd go. But he wouldn't even look at it. He just doesn't care about anything. I give up."

Allan said that he and his wife had seen the problems even in kindergarten. But Kyle was so cute and charming then that he could get away with it. Everyone said he'd grow out of it. He didn't. And it wasn't cute anymore in 3rd grade, or 5th grade, or junior high, where he finally got expelled for being disruptive.

Kyle's parents felt so alone and frustrated. The person at school who expelled Kyle said that he had ADHD. His parents wondered why, if the school knew the problem was ADHD, they expelled him anyway.

Kyle was then formally diagnosed with ADHD. He seemed to have every single symptom. They tried medication—Concerta and others—but Kyle hated taking it, and it made him act like a zombie. For a brief period of time, the medication seemed to allow Kyle to get his homework done, but after awhile, it didn't seem to be effective anymore. Not really liking any medications, Allan didn't feel right about forcing his son to take drugs that he didn't want to take.

"I don't understand him," Allan said. "I'm just so curious and interested in everything. I want to know about everything. If I need to get something done, I just go after it and do it. My wife is like that, too. Kyle isn't interested in anything. He just doesn't care. He's an exceptional drummer. He's had two drum instructors tell him that he should get in a band. But, no, he doesn't want to.

He used to be really hyper and all over the place when he was little. Now he doesn't do anything. His older brother is gifted, and his younger sister does great in school. That's got to be making Kyle feel even worse."

Allan shared that they had had a 504 Plan (an Accommodation Plan for students who are at-risk for failure but not in special education) at school so that Kyle could have certain accommodations made for him in his classes. "It didn't work. Nobody followed through or cared." Allan voiced the frustration that there were so many professionals out there, all with different answers, but nothing had worked. No one really knew what to do. No one really got it.

People who don't have attention problems themselves often find it impossible to understand that there really are some people who cannot pay attention. They may be able to accept it intellectually but cannot get it emotionally, so they continue to view the resulting behaviors as disruptive, unmotivated, uncaring, and unacceptable. This was the case for Kyle's teachers and even for Allan, he admitted. "How can someone *not* be able to pay attention if he wants to?"

What started out in our conversation as a tough, "I've had it; I'm done with this," attitude was morphing into what it really was: years and years of heartache and concern, feelings of inadequacy, the feeling of being helpless and alone, and yet, knowing he couldn't give up on his son.

Confusing pieces of advice

Alisha did fine in first and second grade. At least her teachers thought so. But Alisha's mom, Georgia, had this niggling feeling that things weren't going quite as smoothly as Alisha's report cards indicated. Alisha had to be coaxed and prodded to do her homework, and her mom had to be right there with her coaching on every word or problem. Was this OK? Is this how first and second graders do their homework?

By third grade, tears and tantrums began replacing Alisha's reluctance to do homework. Georgia began to mention to family and close friends that maybe Alisha had a learning problem. That's when the barrage of confusing and conflicting information began pouring in.

"Relax, she'll be fine!"

"Ask the school to test her for special education."

"Hey, I struggled in school and I made it. She just needs to work a little harder." "There's nothing wrong with my granddaughter. Let her be a kid. She'll grow out this."

All these well-meaning pieces of advice made Georgia wonder if she was over-reacting or perhaps not doing enough.

Don't believe everything you are told or read.

Terri went straight to the internet when she began to suspect that her son might have a learning disability. It was pretty discouraging because most of what she read told her that her son was going to be stuck with this for life. There were lots of suggestions for accommodating learning problems, but wasn't there something she could do to fix it?

Ron's ten-year-old son was a bit klutzy, highly distractible, and very inconsistent in his performance on school and homework. Ron decided to seek professional advice. He found that there are many fields related to learning including speech therapy, occupational therapy, psychology, developmental optometry, tutoring centers, specialized learning centers, educational therapy, special education, and regular classroom education.

Not all fields are well-understood by the professional in the other specialties, so Ron came away from his quest feeling confused by what felt like polar opposite opinions. What was the right path for *his* son? Would one kind of therapy be enough? If not, where should he begin? Would any of this really work?

There are many options, but which one is right for your child?

We have run into a number of parents over the years who have felt so frantic yet overwhelmed by the options for getting their children help that they have literally jumped from one therapy to another, every month or two. These parents and children usually come away disappointed because nothing has worked. They've tried everything, but didn't stick with anything long enough to make a real difference.

Public schools have services for children with learning disabilities. There are usually at least two levels of service. One level is placement in a special education classroom, which has a smaller class size and a specially credentialed teacher. Another level is for the child to remain in the regular classroom but get support in various ways from a special education teacher or aide.

In addition, speech therapy, occupational therapy, and adaptive physical education may be available. In order to qualify for help through one of these programs, students generally need to show a *very* large discrepancy between their intellectual ability and their actual performance.

Special education services are typically aimed at helping students in four significant ways:

1. Teaching them more slowly or with different materials or modalities so that they can access the curriculum more easily
2. Providing a lower teacher-student ratio and a more accommodating learning environment

3. Providing support to help students keep up with their regular classroom assignments
4. Helping the classroom teacher accommodate the child's needs by providing information, materials, and equipment

Parents often express disillusionment with special education. They expected it to solve the problem, but their child continues to need help year after year. Special education can serve a valuable function in the lives of children, but it is important to have perspective on what it does and doesn't do. Special education focuses adult attention on the child and helps him navigate and manage in the school environment better than he otherwise might. It supports him with accommodations and extra, individualized instruction on class work and curriculum. It may provide some remediation of basic academic skills, particularly at the elementary school level.

Children need to learn reading, writing, spelling, math, history, and a multitude of other subject areas. This is a big job. This is what schools do. What they typically don't do is work below the level of these content areas to train the brain to pay attention and process information more effectively. They generally do not have the funding, training, or time to provide this kind of specialized programming.

Parents have to enter the realm of special education with the understanding that it may provide valuable *support* for their child, but specialized outside help will probably be needed to *solve* the learning problems that are causing the child to need support in the first place.

Often, a child is clearly struggling in school but doesn't qualify for special education services. What this usually means is that the child is compensating well enough that he isn't as drastically behind as he needs to be in order to be considered a part of the 5–9 percent of children who are diagnosed with a learning disability. It doesn't mean that there isn't a problem, that the child is lazy, or that the parent is crazy. It just means he didn't meet the specific guidelines required.

One option that may be available for the child is what is called a 504 Plan. This is an "Accommodation Plan" for students who are in danger of failing but don't qualify for special education. Parents, the student, and school personnel can work together to create a list of accommodations that may help the student be more successful in class. This may include such things as:

- Being able to use a digital recorder in class or have a note-taker for lectures
- Getting a copy of the of the teacher's PowerPoint slides or notes
- Having extra time on tests or being able to take tests orally
- Having fewer spelling words or reducing the length or complexity of assignments
- Sitting in the front of the class for better attention or support for listening or seeing, and
- Having an assignment sheet that the teacher signs-off on daily to confirm that all of the homework is written down properly.

This can be a very individualized list, which should be carefully developed with everyone's input. Because the child with a 504 Plan isn't formally diagnosed, and because learning and attention challenges can be misunderstood by those who don't have them, parents and older students must be very pro-active about making sure that the accommodations agreed upon in the 504 Plan are carried out.

Parents may find that working closely with an understanding teacher will be easier and just as effective a having a formal 504 Plan, but either way, it is important to remember that accommodations are helpful, but they are not a permanent solution. No one wants to spend their life just finding ways around their challenges. Use a 504 Plan or teacher accommodations as a support while the real problem is being addressed.

Whether or not a student qualifies for special help or accommodations at school, parents of children with learning and attention challenges typically find themselves spending a great deal of time trying to re-teach, organize, and do homework with their child. This can become a serious stressor on the family, particularly if the parent and child are not seeing the kinds of results they would expect from their efforts.

Is home schooling the answer?

Jacob and his mom were an excellent home schooling team. Jacob was a willing learner, and his mom was a patient and thorough teacher. But by the time Jacob was in 7th grade, both he and his parents were concerned, because in spite of all their efforts, he struggled to get complete information when listening and was easily overwhelmed with reading and spelling. Home schooling had been a very good option for Jacob, allowing him to achieve in spite of learning challenges, but it was not resolving the challenges.

After working with Jacob and his mom to provide him with a specialized program to improve his auditory processing skills and overall learning efficiency, Jacob's mom had this to say:

"I cannot tell you how thrilled we continue to be in seeing the changes in Jacob. We have seen a dramatic change in his work in school as well as him as a person. Today he wrote a two-paragraph summary that in the past would have taken three days to write. It took him one hour with no help from anyone. And no tears or frustration. Yesterday, he read to me out of his science book (his most high-level text), and it was so smooth and effortless, I thought I might cry! We (including Jacob) are on cloud nine here."

Can tutoring help?

Many families seek traditional tutoring when their child is struggling in school. Unfortunately, if tutoring is used to treat a learning or attention problem, it is likely to end up being a never-ending proposition.

Tutoring typically focuses on academic skills or school subjects. In most cases, learning problems are the result of weak or incompletely developed learning skills. Traditional tutoring *assumes* that these underlying learning skills are in place. Working on the academics without a solid foundation of learning/processing skills is like spinning your wheels. It may cause students to wonder what is wrong with them that they always have to have tutoring and can never seem to learn to do the job on their own.

Tutoring may provide a way to help students get their homework done. But it can also become a crutch because it doesn't really solve the problem so that the student can do his homework on his own. Many parents have said to me, "My child has had tutoring on and off over the years. He seems to do OK when we've got a tutor, but as soon as we quit, things go downhill again."

The tutor's presence and specific guidance are filling in the gaps in the student's attention, memory, and thinking, allowing the student to be more successful. But because the student needs the tutor to make up for his areas of weak underlying learning skills, he may not be able to be successful on his own.

Tutoring is most effective as a solution to a *short-term* problem. When our son was in 10th grade, he transferred from a very mediocre high school to a very high achieving high school. He got into an Advanced Placement Algebra 2 class that was way over his head. We got him a tutor and after six or eight weeks, he began to get things sorted out. This was a short-term problem with a short-term solution.

Katy, a student with a history of difficulty with math, had a different problem. She had learned to do math by rote memory and lots of painful effort. But she didn't really understand how numbers work. She could easily mix up math processes or steps and not realize it. Or she might recognize her error but not know how to fix it.

When Katy got into algebra, she was lost. And no amount of tutoring was going to clear up the issue because Katy did not have the underlying concepts or thinking skills that were absolutely critical to her success. A long-term learning problem must be dealt with by getting at the underlying issues.

Don't let your child "fall through the cracks."

One of the things I dread hearing a parent say is, "School just isn't his thing." That might be true, but a student with good foundational learning skills, can still get an education, even if school isn't his favorite thing. Students with poor learning skills who are allowed to fall through the cracks, may continue the pattern of "not doing that well" into an adulthood of underachievement and difficulty finding and holding a job. With fewer and fewer blue-collar options in our society today, we don't want our children to enter adulthood uneducated. It limits their options, and in too many cases, gets in the way of them being the productive, independent, fulfilled men and women that they have the potential to be.

Our prisons are full of bright, uneducated people and have a much higher percentage of people with learning disabilities than the typical adult population. Learning disabilities and attention deficits do not have to be the deciding factor in a person's success or failure. In most cases, building and retraining the underlying learning skills can correct these challenges.

What is the cost to fix the problem?
What price does your child pay to not fix it?

One afternoon, sitting at the ice skating rink while my daughter was in lessons, another parent shared with me that her daughter was dyslexic. We got to talking about how dyslexia could be corrected. She asked how much it cost and said, "How can anyone afford that?" My thought was, "How can anyone not?" This mom's solution to her daughter's dyslexia was to build up her self-esteem with something else: ice skating lessons.

Great! By all means help your children find things to do that they're good at or that make them feel good. But don't ignore the challenge that will chip away at their self-esteem and future, every single day. Self-esteem is built on real skills. When a dyslexic child begins to feel like a reader, there is no way to describe the change in her confidence and view of herself.

Medication is not a permanent solution.

Somewhere along the road of trying to find help for their children, most parents will encounter the question of medication. Joshua, a very bright five-year-old boy was having difficulty in kindergarten. He had an inflexible and demanding teacher who was not at all a match for Joshua's creative personality and already evident dyslexic challenges. Joshua became very anxious about his performance at school and had a few meltdowns. His doctor suggested putting him on antidepressants. What? He's five! He's dyslexic, misunderstood, and over-placed in a first grade class masquerading as a kindergarten. Of course he's anxious.

There may be a place for medication at times, but it is not "the answer." There is no magic pill. It must be understood that while drugs might cover or control the symptoms, they don't teach children to read and they rarely address the real issues causing the learning, attention, and behavior problems.

There are permanent, non-drug solutions.

Most learning and attention problems can be largely overcome or completely and permanently solved through a process of neurodevelopmental learning skills training. Neurodevelopmental learning skills encompass a whole continuum of skills that help us take-in, think about, organize, and use information for learning. These are the skills that come before academics. They are rarely taught, but provide the crucial foundation upon which academic learning is built.

The first step is to identify what underlying learning skills are not developed or functional enough to support efficient learning. Then these areas are developed through focused, intensive, cognitive (brain) training programs and strategies. Once the brain is ready and available for learning, the basic academic skills such as reading, writing, and math can be successfully and much more easily taught.

Rafael was a student with severe auditory and language processing delays and accompanying challenges in attention and reading. Without specialized learning skills training, followed by remediation in reading and language, Rafael was headed for a life of being dependent and most likely unemployable. When one of our staff ran into him years after his training at the learning center, Rafael was a pharmacist.

If you are a parent of a child who struggles in school, you may have come to a point on your journey where you feel helpless and hopeless. You may feel alone, like you're the only one stumbling down this difficult road. You may have tried so many things and spent so much money that you just want to give up. But you don't. Because it's your kid. As you read the next few chapters, I hope you will get a better understanding of how learning works, see what the solutions to learning challenges look like, and be encouraged. There are answers.

Action items. . .
- Go to www.LearningDisability.com.
  Under "Free Articles," read:
    * "Sometimes It Takes More than a Tutor."
    * "Does My Child Need Educational Therapy?"
    * "We Get Questions."
- Go to www.FixLearningSkills.com.
    * Listen to "Sometimes It Takes More than a Tutor."

———————————————————●———

CHAPTER 5

How Learning Works

*What are the 7 systems that can
make or break easy, successful learning?*

In this chapter. . .

- How lack of physical control interferes with learning
- Why the ability to process information properly is key to effortless learning
- What attention awareness and control have to do with both learning and classroom behavior
- How memory and the ability to manage behavior, organize thinking, and evaluate the outcome of decisions affect development

**For optimal learning, many different
skills work together automatically.**

Imagine a tree. Your eye is probably drawn to the top of the tree with its full display of branches and leaves. This is the most noticeable part of the tree, but of course, the branches and leaves cannot thrive without a strong trunk and root system below to support them.

Now think about learning. Most likely, the first thought that comes to mind involves school subjects such as reading, math, sciences, foreign language, and history. Academic skills are like the top of the tree: important, visible, but only part of the picture.

Let's consider what a typical successful student looks like. We'll start with the obvious: good grades. Now let's look a little deeper. This is an intelligent high school student with a good sense of time so that he can get to class before the bell rings. He has good control over his body so that he can walk to his desk without bumping into other people or things. He knows exactly where he's going and can see the most efficient way to get there. When he gets to his seat, he can easily manage his materials and has the stamina and control to sit with good posture through the whole period.

Our successful student uses his mental inner language to remind himself to get out his homework because it has to be turned in the first five minutes of class. He doesn't waste any time digging through his backpack because he always puts his completed homework in the same spot in his folder. He also gets out his book, paper for notes, and a pencil. He knows that his teacher starts right away, and he'll miss something if he doesn't have his materials ready.

Our successful student has good listening and attention skills, so he can easily get the information the teacher is lecturing about and simultaneously organize his thoughts and write down the most relevant points. Handwriting and spelling are automatic for him, so he does not have to divert any extra energy toward thinking about them.

Even though there are noises outside and some other students whispering in the back of the class, our successful student can block out unimportant sounds and keep focused on the teacher. He is not distracted by things he sees in the classroom, even though the bulletin boards and displays are very colorful.

Our student can quickly understand what he sees, so when the teacher refers to a chart in the textbook, our student feels no confusion and can locate it right away.

Our student is confident and can express himself well, so he easily participates in discussions and impresses his teachers and classmates with his insight. When it's time to begin class work, our student knows exactly what to do because his memory skills are strong, and he can quickly remember not only the directions, but other similar tasks that he has done before in class. He is able to get started right away because he is focused and chooses to do so because he's getting together with friends that afternoon and doesn't want to have any extra homework. He mentally calculates the amount of class time available and adjusts his energy, attention, and working speed so that he can complete the work by the end of class.

When our successful student begins to read his textbook, his eyes move across the page smoothly, noticing each word and moving fluidly to the next line without losing his place. No conscious energy goes into his eyes working together easily to see the words or into sounding out the words. He is able to do these things so automatically that they never divert his attention from comprehending the material.

It may sound silly to look at student behaviors this way, but this is what easy, efficient learning is all about. The physical and mental skills needed to learn are in place at an automatic level, so all the student really has to focus on is the material. Learners with these skills get to enjoy school and have energy left over for extra-curricular activities and time with friends. Their energy is not being siphoned off by having to spend too much of it trying to listen, focus on the page, pay attention, understand, or sit in the chair. Their confidence is not being eroded by feeling out of control.

This marvelous skill set that allows for comfortable efficient learning falls on a continuum of what we call neurodevelopmental learning skills. We are going to look at these skills in terms of seven systems that can make or break easy, successful learning.

System 1: The motor system and body control

The movements that a baby makes shortly after birth are not well thought out controlled movements but rather the result of reflexes. With the help of these reflex movements and the developing brain, babies begin to move more intentionally. Growth and development naturally follows a path of greater awareness and control of the muscles and the body, and finer and more sophisticated movements and thinking.

By the time a child gets to school, it is assumed that he has control of his body and movements so that he is ready for the social, attentional, and academic demands of the classroom. If the progression of motor (muscle control and movement) development does not occur as it should, it may interfere with easy, efficient learning.

Manny attended a highly academic private school. In 4th grade, Manny had all of the basic academic skills needed to be successful.

What Manny didn't have was stamina or body control. He literally lay on his desk as limp as a rag doll. He had no energy in his voice and his hand was so limp he could barely hold a pencil. Because Manny had good reading and math skills, his posture and lack of interest looked like a choice.

The truth was that Manny's intelligence had allowed him to learn higher-level skills, but his lower-level skills of body awareness and motor control had not developed as they should. The weaknesses in early neurodevelopmental learning skills kept him from having the support he needed to function successfully. He was literally like the top of a tree without most of its roots.

System 2: Visual processing

Do you recall that our successful student was able to read his textbook with no extra effort, strain, or attention on his eyes? What if we took that same student, but this time when he looks at the page, he sees individual letters but doesn't "see" the white spaces between words or that the letters are clumped together into groups? What if his eyes didn't notice the beginning of words but just went back and forth trying to put together enough letters to read.

Now our student is working extremely hard both visually and mentally to try to piece together enough information to make sense out of what he is seeing. Instead of reading the chapter by the end of the class period, our student will have read a half a page if he's lucky. At this rate, he will probably no longer qualify to be our successful student.

Early visual skills development is aided by the reflex movements that babies make. If all goes well, the child's eyes will be ready by about age seven or eight to automatically perform tasks such as:

1. Working together to move fluidly across a line of text, noticing each word and all of the letters in it,
2. Easily moving from one line to the next without darting away or losing their place,
3. Focusing up close or in the distance, easily shifting back and forth as is needed for copying from the board,

4. Following a moving object or person, such as a ball to be caught or a teacher who is moving while talking,

5. Moving accurately from one spot to the next, as is needed for reading and looking from speaker to speaker in a discussion or conversation,

6. Noticing fine visual detail and being able to tell the difference between symbols that look similar, such as b, d, p, and q; h and n; t and f; and saw and was.

Weaknesses in any of these skills can cause a learner to have to expend a great deal more energy than she should on many school related tasks. This takes energy away from attention and learning.

Christy is a good student in college, but she never reads by choice and dreads the hours and hours she has to spend studying. She finds herself avoiding opening textbooks until she absolutely has to. Her vision is 20/20, but her eyes are not working together well to focus on the words on the page. This causes reading to be so stressful and taxing that she becomes sleepy almost immediately when she starts to read.

Visual skills develop to a very sophisticated level and are highly involved with thinking and learning. Being able to "see a movie in our head" as we read a good book, envision something we want to build or create, or "see" things from different angles or a different point of view are all skills that are connected with our visual processing system.

System 3: Auditory processing

Listening skills, or auditory processing skills, also have a profound impact on functioning and learning. When I met Alita, she was seven-years-old and already had quite a history. She had been suspended from school five times. She was aggressive and pushed and hit others often. She appeared unteachable and would not do any of the work in her special education class unless her aide was sitting right there virtually doing it for her. Alita's speech was unintelligible, and she screamed more than she talked. She lashed out with extreme frustration when given tasks she couldn't do. Since she did not have the underlying learning skills she needed for even the simplest reading or math readiness tasks, she was constantly being pushed beyond her tolerance level. She looked, acted, and was treated like a "behavior problem child."

Alita's real problem was a severe auditory processing delay that left her feeling completely lost in the world, with no appropriate way to communicate. Even though Alita could hear, the messages she was getting when listening were garbled and unclear. She couldn't understand much of what people were saying, and because she had never processed words and language clearly, she couldn't reproduce them in her own speech.

After twenty weeks of intensive Auditory Stimulation and Training, Alita was like a completely different child. She had a long way to go academically, but because she was able to hear language more clearly, she also began to use language instead of screaming or pushing. Her speech became easier for others to understand, and she was able to follow directions more easily, now that she could make sense out of what she was hearing. Alita's teacher found that Alita could participate in the class on most days and was actually learning.

The auditory processing system has neurological connections to every organ in the body except the spleen. It works very closely with the vestibular system, or sense of balance and movement, as well as the parts of the brain that regulate attention, energy, emotions, language, thinking, and learning. As a result, weaknesses in auditory processing can impact a person's:

Speech	Attention
Reading	Coordination
Comprehension	Energy
Communication	Creativity
Learning	Organization
Emotional Balance	Sense of Self
Sleep	Sense of Well-Being
Relationships	

How we function in the world is highly dependent upon our listening skills. Our relationships, communication, and learning are directly related to our response to sound. It can be assumed that, if a child's listening skills are weak, he is under his potential for learning and processing information.

System 4: Language processing

Adam was considered mentally retarded. He was fifteen, but he didn't speak much; only one or two words at a time that sounded more like grunts than words. He was a tall boy with poor posture, who had low energy and a history of a combative attitude, though we never saw it. For Adam to write even a single sentence was painfully difficult. He couldn't think of what to say or how to spell the words. He used poor grammar and very simple vocabulary.

He had an extremely short attention span, but as long as he wasn't causing trouble, he was generally ignored at school. Since he didn't talk much and didn't comprehend well, people just assumed he was doing the best he could.

Adam had a number of learning skills deficits that were addressed simultaneously and intensively when he started at the learning center in June, but key to his remarkable transformation was the work with auditory and language processing. As Adam began to get more complete and accurate information through his auditory system, he was more mentally available and ready to improve his language comprehension and expressive language.

Adam's mom was very observant about the changes in Adam's language and the impact they were having on his life, as seen in the notes below that help chronicle his progress:

July: Adam's behaviorist reported that Adam seemed a lot friendlier than he used to be, was volunteering more information, and was using much more exact wording. For example, Adam commented one day, when he had a headache, "My mom said I have to hydrate more." Adam's mom noticed that Adam was using "normal intonation and volume" more often.

September: Adam's mom reported, "Adam had the third highest score on his World History test out of the entire class, got student of the week, and is doing wonderfully in his P.E. class."

November: E-mail observations from Adam's mom: "I want you all to know that this was the first time <u>ever</u> that Adam sat at the Thanksgiving dinner table and actually conversed with all the adult guests and relatives for over an hour, many times directly in relation to questions/comments being made to him, then interjected in other conversations when appropriate to offer a comment or question. I have never seen him sustain this attention or length of conversation ever before.

"He is picking up more conversation, has fewer 'huhs,' and is expressing himself with wider vocabulary. In fact, in the conversation, he used words I had never heard him use before. A couple of times, he 'searched' for words and he found them!!! You could see him searching in his mind, but instead of filling in a simpler word, or using 'that thing' or 'you know, when you do this, like that' etcetera, he actually [stuck with it and] found the words. This is really different for Adam."

As Adam's language processing has improved, his demeanor and communication have drastically changed. Adam is now very chatty and interactive, very interested in current events, has made friends from the "regular education" population, and has been able to respond well to academic remediation of reading, spelling, written language, and math. Adam's diagnosis of mental retardation is now in question.

Doing well in school and functioning well in society relies heavily on being able to understand and use language. Language processing depends upon getting good information from the auditory and visual systems, as well as understanding the messages coming in. Language has many layers of complexity, starting with being able to say and understand speech sounds, words, and word parts, and moving all the way to understanding very abstract ideas and vocabulary. Body language, vocal intonation, and intent of the speaker all contribute to a person's overall understanding of language.

Being able to understand spoken and written language is critical to learning, problem solving, and relationships. Being able to express our ideas with the right words, grammar, intensity, sequence, and flow is critical to being heard and showing what we know.

System 5: Attention awareness and control

Attention is so basic to learning that it almost goes without saying that problems with attention awareness and control will result in challenges in school. Students with attention challenges do not necessarily have learning problems; although, lack of attention could cause interference to gaining needed academic skills.

Allan's son, Kyle, who we met in Chapter 4, had the academic skills to do the work. What he didn't have was the sustained attention to sit through a class without getting bored. "Boredom" is a classic symptom of the person's attention system not being aroused enough to keep him attentive. As a little boy, Kyle kept himself awake by popping up and down out of his seat and talking out all the time. When he became a teenager, his "boredom" led to low energy, apathy, and lack of follow-through. He's quit trying now, because even his good intentions always turn out the same. He can't get himself going and can't keep his mind on what he's doing.

In spite of all of the publicity that Attention Deficit Disorder (ADD) and Attention Deficit Hyperactivity Disorder (ADHD) have received, they are hard to understand. These kids often don't respond to either rewards or punishment. Kyle's dad offered to buy him a truck when he was sixteen if he'd follow through with taking his driver's test, but Kyle didn't do it. This is not lack of motivation. This is the result of attention that is not in his control.

System 6: Memory

Memory, like attention, is one of the most basic ingredients of learning. It affects virtually every area of learning. Two key components of memory are the ability to take in enough information at one time and the ability to use inner language to hold onto it. Inner language can be visual (using visualization to retain information), or verbal (actually "hearing" it in your mind to remember and work through information).

As people age, they begin to joke about senior moments when they can't remember names, words, or where they put things. In those who are not yet having senior moments, memory challenges may be mistaken for other issues. Here are some examples:

Johnny is having trouble learning to read. He can only remember two things at a time, but most of the words in first grade have four or five letters. His weak memory span is getting in the way of remembering words and sounds for reading.

Susie is having trouble learning to read, too. Her visual memory is not strong enough to retain a stable image of the letters, so she can't always recognize them, and she gets confused when she looks at the page.

Carol misses bits and pieces of information in class lectures because she can't take in and store the information as fast as her teacher speaks. She feels like she's always trying to "connect the dots."

Vince is notorious for getting lost. He has trouble picturing and remembering how streets are laid out. He also tends to overbook himself because he doesn't carry a mental image of his calendar in his head.

Sara often cuts in line and jumps into games on the playground before it's her turn. She has visual memory issues that have caused her to fail to observe the basic rules and flow of playground games. Other kids get mad at her, but she doesn't really understand why.

Karrie has trouble reading, spelling, and expressing herself because she gets sounds and words out of sequence.

The challenges that all of these students are experiencing are related to poor auditory or visual memory skills.

System 7: Executive function

Lauren is hanging out with friends in the quad after school. She looks at her watch and says to herself, "It's 3:40 and I have swim practice at 4:00. I'd better head over to the gym now to change, or I'll be late getting in the pool." This is her executive function speaking.

Executive function is like our personal manager. It is the highest level of awareness and control. Executive function is needed in order for us to mentally talk ourselves through problems and monitor and guide our decisions and behavior. It also serves a "How's it working for you?" function. Was the decision a good one? Did the behavior work out as planned? If not, our executive function allows us to think about other options and try a new way next time. Children who are very rigid and inflexible, among other things, have challenges with executive function.

Executive function also facilitates our ability to direct and sustain our attention. Even though Sarah is hungry and bored in her history class, her good executive function skills allow her to sit up taller, focus on the teacher, and say to herself, "The teacher said this would be important for the test, so I'd better pay attention." A student in the same class with poor executive function skills might turn to another student and say, too loudly, "Man, this is so boring. Can't we just get out of here already?" Executive function helps us to inhibit our reactions and restrain or delay responses.

The good "student" behaviors we like to see in our children, particularly in middle school and high school, such as planning out long-term projects, using a planner or assignment sheet, strategizing how to organize and complete the night's homework, problem solving, note-taking, and test-taking strategies all fall under the category of executive function. This function of the brain continues to develop well into adulthood. As executive function grows, the child will appear more and more mature.

In Conclusion

A weakness in one or more of these learning systems – motor and body awareness and control, visual processing, auditory processing, language processing, attention awareness and control, memory, or executive function – will make school more difficult than it would otherwise be, even with strong intelligence and good compensating strategies. The good news is that none of these systems is static. With specific and intensive training, the brain can learn to work more efficiently in all of these areas.

Action items. . .
- Go to www.LearningDisability.com.
  Under "Free Articles," read:
    * Not Learning Disabled, but Learning Abled."

CHAPTER 6

Addressing the Problem
at the Source, the Brain

What current brain plasticity research says about changing the
brain and how brain training can help children with
learning and attention challenges

In this chapter. . .

- How the brain processes information is key to learning
- Research proves that the brain can change and processing, or learning skills, can improve
- How correcting processing issues can lead to rapid improvement in attitudes, relationships, and grades
- Who can benefit from improved brain processing ability?

Poor processing of sensory input sabotages learning.

At eleven years old, Evan could not speak more than a word or two at a time. He did not even seem to be aware of when people in the room were speaking. Evan was not mentally retarded or deaf, but his behavior was similar to that of a two-year-old who could not hear. He communicated mainly with noises. He ran from room to room in the learning center, interrupting and disregarding any instruction. He was boisterous and volatile.

Evan had severe auditory and language processing delays. He had gotten through school so far in a special class with his own aide, who sat with him and essentially did his work for him. He had extreme attention problems and didn't appear to be able to learn.

Evan began an intensive program of Auditory Stimulation and Training and Core Learning Skills Training to improve his auditory processing, or listening skills, and his body and attention awareness and control. And he began to learn. Evan can now express himself with clear enough articulation and language that he can easily be understood. He has learned to read and enjoys it. He loves writing simple stories. He plays soccer and can now actually be part of the team, knowing where the ball is and where he should be.

After eleven years of virtually no language and comprehension, why was Evan finally able to learn? Or maybe the right question to ask is, why wasn't he able to learn in the first place?

You can't build a brick wall if you don't have any bricks. You can't build speech and reading if you don't have any sounds. Evan's brain couldn't "hear" the sounds in words because his auditory processing was not providing him with the information he needed. By re-training the brain to listen, Evan then had the bricks that he needed to begin to build language.

A surprising breakthrough revealed that the brain could be retrained.

In the mid 1970s, Patricia Lindamood, speech pathologist, teacher, researcher, and author, made a groundbreaking discovery about reading.[1] She found that the reason people had trouble learning to read was not because they couldn't see the letters and words properly or because they had bad teachers or reading programs. It was because they could not process, or think about, the sounds inside of words. It was like they couldn't "hear" the sounds. This is the thinking process that supports learning and using phonics for reading and spelling. It didn't matter if these people had the best phonics programs and the best phonics teachers in the world; if the brain couldn't hear the sounds, they could not learn and use phonics effectively.

What Pat Lindamood also discovered was that through very specific and intensive training, the brain could develop new neuropathways or ways to process information. She could actually retrain the brain to think about the sounds in words. This removed the roadblock to learning to read.

Pat Lindamood was ahead of her time. Her idea that intensive training could actually create new neuropathways, or connections in the brain, has now been proven through brain research. Dr. Michael Merzenich, a neuroscientist at the University of California, San Francisco, proved that the brain makes actual physical changes in response to training.[2] This ability of the brain to reorganize or rewire itself and make new connections is called brain plasticity.

This is a powerful discovery because it validates what we have seen for more than two decades working with children and adults with learning challenges. Brain function can be improved. Norman Doidge, M.D. says in his book, *The Brain that Changes Itself,* "Before Merzenich's work, the brain was seen as a complex machine, having unalterable limits on memory, processing speed, and intelligence. Merzenich has shown that each of these assumptions is wrong."[3]

One of the best things about neuroplasticity is that it is drug free. The dramatic changes in thinking, brain function, and abilities occur through training in targeted, repetitive, challenging activities.

Parents are ever hopeful that things will get better. By the time they call our center for help, there is often a sense of desperation that maybe it's too late. It is thought that children learn things most easily at certain ages, that the brain is most receptive within certain windows of time. While there are optimal windows for learning certain kinds of things, we now know that it is never too late for the brain to be retrained to learn a new way.

It's never too late.

Linc was fifty-one when he broke down and called the learning center for an assessment. Linc was smart and capable with his hands. He was good with people, so in each job he'd had, he'd been encouraged to move up to a management position. Linc knew he didn't dare because he would never be able to handle the paperwork and someone might find out his humiliating secret. Eventually, Linc would quit and move on to another entry-level job in order to avoid the pressure to move into management.

When I met Linc, he had given up on working for someone else, figuring that owning his own business would solve the paperwork problem. Then the government began requiring more and more paperwork from small business owners. Linc was completely dependent on his wife, a first grade teacher, to complete it. Finally, Linc had had enough. At his wife's insistence, he came to his testing appointment, head down, shoulders rounded in embarrassment. The appointment was short. Linc couldn't read or spell. Period.

He went through a program of remediation to retrain his brain to process, or think about the sounds in words. Once the brain had the information it needed, Linc was able to learn to read. I will never forget the day he told me he had asked his wife to bring home a book from her first grade classroom and he had read it. He said, "You can't even imagine how it feels to read a book. I know it's just a simple first grade book to you, but to me, it is freedom." It may be hard to muster the courage to call for help, but the brain can change. It's never too late.

Attention problems often clear up when the processing problem is solved.

I started the learning center long before ADHD became the buzzword. At the time, I didn't know much about Attention Deficit Disorder, but what I did know was that the vast majority of our students had attention problems. We were much more skilled at solving learning problems than attention problems in those days at the center, so we focused on what we could do. Time after time, we found that as the learning problems cleared up, the attention challenges disappeared as well.

This is not to say that there is no such thing as ADHD. We know now that there is, and in spite of good academic skills, it can be just as devastating to school success as a learning disability. But the message here is that if any of our learning skills are stressed or not working for us as well as they should, our attention, and generally memory as well, will be stressed. The extra energy and attention needed to perform has to come from somewhere, causing other areas to suffer.

There are many hints that a processing issue is the problem.

Byron is a very functional, successful adult who is an asset to his company. But Byron has auditory processing problems. It takes a tremendous amount of energy to listen. Since listening is so hard, he also has to put extra energy into paying attention to the speaker. Byron says that listening is so exhausting for him, that after a one-hour meeting, he's wiped out. He has to go to his office and take a nap.

James has trouble sitting in his chair. He wants to be really good so he tries really hard to sit still when the teacher says to. He doesn't get his papers done, though, because all of his attention and energy is going into not wiggling and staying in his seat.

Kara has trouble reading the words in her book. It's so hard that she has to keep looking away. When she gets to the end of the page, she has no idea what the story was about because all of her attention went into figuring out the words.

Processing problems can affect social skills.

The underlying learning skills that we need for academics are also the skills that support our social life. Problems with attention, memory, auditory or visual processing, processing speed, body awareness and control, or executive function (the organizing and problem solving part of the brain) can cause difficulties with relationships.

Kelly was actually a very popular girl. She was a good student and a cheerleader. But beneath the surface, she felt lost. Kelly had memory challenges that made it difficult for her to follow and participate well in conversations. She knew how to smile and be sweet, all the while hanging quietly on the edge of the conversation. When Kelly went through some memory training that helped her to visualize and use her inner language better, she very quickly saw a difference in herself.

Four weeks after starting her program at the learning center, she came in very excited, saying, "I was able to tell my friends all about the dress I bought for the prom! I just pictured it in my mind, and I could remember everything about it! I've never been able to tell anyone about things I've bought or done before!"

Nick was a very quiet, compliant boy who never asked questions when he didn't understand, never fought with his siblings, and never talked back. When he began his auditory stimulation and training program, he began to find his voice. Once he could process what he was hearing better, he had something to say. "No!" Nick began talking back and fighting with his sister. Not exactly the result his parents were looking for. But Nick also began to ask his teacher for help. He began to do better in school and made new friends.

Children need to learn how to say no and how to express their needs and opinions. It's an important part of finding out who they are, and standing up for themselves. Kids have to find their voice. Parents have to guide them in knowing how to use it appropriately.

Removing the roadblocks and retraining the brain makes learning easier.

At the learning center, we provide neurodevelopmental learning skills training. We look to see what underlying learning skills are not supporting the student well enough, and we remove those roadblocks by retraining the brain to process or think about information more efficiently. Once the barriers to learning are removed, we can remediate the academic skills.

When parents are worried about their child's grades, it's sometimes hard for them to understand why taking the time to build the underlying learning skills is important. Working on schoolwork to get the grades up seems so much more pressing. But working on academic skills when there are lags or barriers to the child understanding those skills is truly an exercise in frustration for everyone involved.

When the roadblocks to learning are removed and the child has the mental tools, the solid base of learning skills, to do the job, he can learn the needed academic skills so much faster and more easily, leading to independence and better grades. Sometimes, improving the learning skills alone is enough to make the difference so that no remediation is needed.

**Correcting the processing skills alone may end
the struggle for some students.**

Michael came to us as an 11th grader attending a very academic private high school. Michael's testing showed that he was four to six years below age level in all areas of reading (decoding, sight words, and comprehension), and weak in memory, processing speed, and auditory and visual processing. He had good reasoning skills and was a motivated student, so in spite of very inefficient processing, he was maintaining Bs in his classes.

Following fifteen hours of processing skills development, Michael was very happy to report that he was now able to take notes in class and keep up with his peers. By the end of his twelve-week (thirty-six-hour) program, Michael's scores and school performance had improved so much that he did not need the reading and comprehension remediation that was initially recommended.

Wes was in a regular 4th grade class, struggling to keep up. Testing showed that his reading was more than two years below grade level, though his comprehension was good. Auditory processing scores were very low for his age. Wes was extremely quiet, and when he spoke his speech was unclear and difficult to understand.

Following Wes' twenty-week Auditory Stimulation and Training program, he scored at grade level in reading, even though he had had no formal reading remediation. His auditory processing improved, and Wes was doing great in school, according to his teacher. It was such fun to see how this very timid, quiet boy had come out of his shell. He was talkative and energized. People no longer had to strain to hear or understand him. Like Michael, Wes did not need the reading remediation that had originally been recommended.

**Success begins with a thorough assessment
that reveals correctable weaknesses.**

Neurodevelopmental learning skills training (learning skills training) has many different components, which fall along a continuum. We will look at the learning continuum in detail in Chapter 7. Following assessment to understand exactly where on the continuum the student's learning skills are breaking down, a program or sequence of programs is recommended to develop and strengthen them. Keys to success in learning skills training are:

1. Start working where the student *is*, not where you want him to be.

2. Instruction should be provided on a one-to-one basis. This allows the instructor to target all of the instruction very specifically for that student. It keeps students from practicing incorrectly because they can get immediate feedback. It allows the instructor to work intensively and at a challenging level for that student.

3. Work intensively. Frequency of instruction as well as focus and intensity during the sessions is critical. Daily instruction or practice is most often recommended or required. I like an analogy Pat Lindamood often used: Imagine that you want to play baseball on a field of grass. You lay down your bases, but there are no pathways between them. If you want to make a solid pathway between the bases, you'll have to run around the bases over and over and over. Cognitive training is literally creating new neuropathways in the brain. This will happen only with intensive, repetitive movements or activities.

4. Work at a challenging level. High-level athletes don't get to a competitive level by working only on the things they know and can do easily. They are constantly pushing themselves to their limits. This is how they learn new skills and get the edge. When we work with students to develop their learning skills, wherever those skills fall on the continuum, we have to work at a challenging level, stretching their limits so that they can develop and keep the skills that will move them closer to being independent learners.

A personalized program addresses individual needs.

The skills on the Learning Skills Continuum are skills that everyone needs. This kind of training is essential for:

- Students with diagnosed learning disabilities and dyslexia
- The 21–25 percent of school age students who don't qualify for help but are underachieving or struggling in school
- Children and adults with brain injury
- Adults who are underachieving or struggling at work because of poor skills or attention
- The elderly population who want to keep their brains sharp.

Learning skills training will benefit people who want to improve relationships and people who want to be quicker, sharper, and at the top of their game. At one of our training workshops, a participant shared that he owned a helicopter pilot school. He felt that the things he was learning in the workshop would be excellent training for the pilots. This is not a one size fits all kind of approach, but because the learning skills continuum is so comprehensive, and because it covers the key underlying skills needed for any kind of learning, it has very broad applications.

Action items. . .
- Go to www.LearningDisability.com.
  Under "Free Articles," read:
  - * "Unblocking the Roadblocks . . . Preparing the Brain to Learn."

CHAPTER 7

The Neurodevelopmental Learning Skills Continuum

*How using the Learning Skills Continuum can break the
cycle of wasted time, tears over homework, and
one more thing that didn't work*

In this chapter. . .
- How certain characteristics or behaviors point to neurodevelopment challenges
- The five key segments of the Learning Skills Continuum
- Why finding where a child is on the Continuum is vitally important

Identifying and solving early development problems first
Red-haired Grayson bounded into our office, awkwardly and a bit out of control, but with a sparkle in his eye. He was charming and engaging but very hard to understand. Grayson has cerebral palsy. When we met him at eleven years old, his mom explained that there were some sounds he couldn't physically make his mouth form. When I first tested Grayson, I had to record the session because his speech was too unclear for me to decipher without listening to it over and over.

Grayson started a program of auditory stimulation and training. After three weeks, he was able to make all of the speech sounds we were told he couldn't physically make, not only in isolation but in words and sentences. At a school meeting, Grayson's speech therapist, who didn't know that he was coming to the learning center, said to his mom, "Have you noticed how much clearer Grayson's speech has become in the last three weeks!"

Grayson had been in speech therapy since he was two years old. Why was he able to make changes in three weeks that he wasn't able to make in nine years of therapy? Had they been doing the wrong thing all those years? No. But they started in the wrong place. They started too high on the continuum. Until Grayson's brain was trained to process or "hear" the challenging sounds, he wasn't able to make them.

When we started working with Chris, he was a gawky, immature, sixteen-year-old with reading, writing, math, and attention challenges. He had a cavalier, "I can do anything I want," attitude that did not endear him to his teachers. Working with Chris was frustrating because when he sat up tall, he immediately could focus, engage, and learn better. Most of the time, however, Chris sat slumped and listless in his chair. His attitude made his poor posture and lack of focus look intentional and disrespectful.

One session, I decided to work with Chris very specifically on his posture. Since, in his eyes, the "principal" was in the room, Chris was on his best behavior. We tried doing lessons sitting in a chair, on a stool, and finally standing. What we discovered was that Chris couldn't maintain his posture for more than a few seconds. As soon as his head went down slightly to look at his book, his shoulders rounded and pulled in. Chris had retained primitive reflexes (more about this in Chapter 8) that involuntarily triggered this movement.

Chris was not making the progress we had expected, not because of attitude, but because we had started working with him too high up on the learning skills continuum. Chris' program was revised to include Core Learning Skills Training to get rid of the primitive reflexes and improve his body awareness and control. What a change! Chris started looking and acting like a sixteen-year-old. His walk smoothed out, his head was up, and he looked people in the eye. He gained better control of his attention, and his academic remediation began to move along more smoothly. Chris still had an attitude, but it came across as less disrespectful and more appropriately humorous.

The Neurodevelopmental Learning Skills Continuum (Learning Skills Continuum) has five segments:

1. Core Learning Skills (reflex integration; motor and visual skills development)
2. Processing Skills (memory, attention, auditory and visual processing, processing speed, comprehension, reasoning)
3. Executive Function
4. Foundational Academic Skills
5. Content areas and higher learning

As you examine the Learning Skills Continuum on the next page, you may notice that there is overlap among the segments. In addition, within each segment, there are higher and lower level skills.

We want students to make as much progress as they can, as fast as they can. We start them at the highest level on the continuum that we think they can handle and benefit from, but we evaluate this very carefully so that students are getting exactly what they need to correct their learning challenges and become independent learners. It may feel like the process will take too long if you have to start at the Core Learning Skills level and work all the way up. And depending upon the number and severity of issues that need to be corrected or developed, it *can* be quite time intensive. However, without careful attention to the underlying skills that need to be addressed, many students will never get there at all.

Students written about in this book have worked at the learning center anywhere from twelve weeks to three years. They have attended as little as one hour a week, with the parents filling in three to four hours a week at home, to as many as fifteen hours a week. Taking the continuum approach to correcting learning problems is extremely individualized, with the goal of bringing each learner to the highest and most independent level their potential allows.

Learning Skills Continuum

The Learning Skills Continuum				
Core Learning Skills	**Processing Skills**	**Executive Function**	**Basic Language and Academic Skills**	**Content Area/Higher Academic**
• Good sensory input • Postural security • Body Awareness • Reflex integration • Interpret tactile, proprioceptive, and motor input • Balance • Motor planning • Bilateral integration • Cross Lateral Integration • Eye-hand coordination • Ocular-motor control • Listening skills • Visual-Spatial perception • Attention awareness and control • Sensorimotor integration	• Attention • Memory • Processing speed • Language • Auditory processing • Phonemic Awareness • Visual processing • Sensorimotor integration • Sequential processing • Simultaneous processing	• Visual Inner Language • Verbal Inner Language • Organization • Time Orientation • Patterns and relationships • Problem solving • Strategizing • Using information • Making connections • Logic and Reasoning • Relevance vs. Non-Relevance • Planning • Study Skills • Test Taking Strategies	• Language ▪ Receptive ▪ Expressive ▪ Articulation ▪ Vocabulary ▪ Comprehension • Reading ▪ Sound-symbol ▪ Phonics ▪ Sight recognition ▪ Morphology ▪ Vocabulary ▪ Comprehension • Writing ▪ Printing/cursive ▪ Spelling ▪ Sentence structure ▪ Grammar ▪ Organization ▪ Composition ▪ Edit / proof • Math ▪ Concepts: Numeration, time, measurement, change, amount ▪ Computation ▪ Problem solving	• Subject areas • Refining and applying basic academic skills • Study Skills
Motor, Visual, Auditory, Language, Attention, Memory, and Executive Function Systems develop and are used with increasing sophistication as one moves up the continuum. Higher level success is dependent upon a solid lower level foundation.				

We are going to look at three students with various types and degrees of challenges to illustrate how the Learning Skills Continuum is used to create a plan for fixing learning skills and correcting foundational academic areas.

Kendall – Age 12
Background and testing

Kendall is an adopted child. She has many challenges with learning, particularly with reading, and doesn't like school. She is very discouraged and does not believe she has the ability to do well. She shows little pride in her work and often doesn't finish.

Testing showed that Kendall had very poor listening skills, weak auditory memory, and extremely weak phonemic awareness, which is an auditory skill that is critical to success in reading. She had difficulty noticing the difference between letters and words that look similar, causing her to feel confused and disoriented when reading. She felt like the words sometimes were moving on the page, and she often substituted, omitted, or added small common sight words such as *the, of,* and *if.* She left off and added endings on words.

All reading skills, including decoding, sight words, and comprehension were weak. Spelling and listening comprehension scores were also low. Kendall showed the presence of retained reflexes (movement patterns from early development that can interfere with higher learning) and core learning skills delays.

How will these challenges affect Kendall's learning?

- Challenges with listening skills and weak auditory memory will affect Kendall's ability to hold onto, analyze, and interpret information she hears. She may not get complete and accurate information to think with, which will affect her comprehension and ability to follow directions.
- Kendall's weak phonemic awareness is going to make it difficult for her to learn phonics for reading and spelling, causing her to have difficulty sounding out new words.
- Having to put extra energy and attention into seeing and reading the words accurately may make it difficult for Kendall to follow and comprehend what she is reading.
- Due to her core learning skills delays, disorientation when reading, and weak auditory processing skills, Kendall will have to work excessively hard to listen, read, and write, which may affect her stamina, motivation, and task completion. These challenges will keep Kendall from performing as

well as she could, and it may look like she is not trying.

- Kendall will experience frustration with learning, which can affect her self-esteem because she is not getting the results that her hard work deserves.

Using the Continuum to determine a course of action for Kendall

Kendall has had a great deal of reading remediation in the past, and she still is far below grade level in all her reading skills. Before attacking the reading remediation again, Kendall's core learning skills and auditory processing delays must be addressed. The combination of Core Learning Skills Training and Auditory Stimulation and Training will help improve stamina, energy, orientation, and visual skills needed for reading. Auditory Stimulation and Training will increase Kendall's phonemic awareness and auditory memory, both of which are needed in order for her to successfully learn and use phonics for reading and spelling.

Following completion of her core learning skills and auditory training, Kendall should be ready to successfully begin reading remediation.

Carolyn – Age 9
Background and testing

Carolyn is a bubbly, engaging 3rd grader. She is a good reader and has good listening skills. Carolyn's parents are concerned mainly about math and organization skills. They shared that Carolyn never seems to be able to find anything in her room, her desk, or her backpack. She has poor printing and poor organization on the page. Words aren't evenly spaced and don't stay in the lines. Math columns never line up and problems seem scattered on the page. She has not been able to memorize her math facts. Carolyn's parents shared that although Carolyn is pleased with her overall performance in school, she is very self-conscious about the challenges she has in math.

Carolyn gave extremely good effort during the testing and had excellent focus and sustained attention. She responded quickly and confidently on tests involving reading or auditory processing. On tests of visual memory, visual processing, or visual reasoning, and all math subtests, Carolyn's responses were very slow, and she appeared quite uncertain, even when her answer was correct.

Carolyn needed a great deal of thinking time on all items and was reluctant to say when she didn't know. She showed inconsistent visual-spatial skills. Analysis of errors showed that she did not always understand the visual organization of what she was looking at, which could affect her comprehension of how math is organized on the page.

Carolyn attempted to do math calculations, but her skills were incomplete and not automatic. It appeared that she did not really understand the steps or processes, but tried hard to apply whatever she remembered. Carolyn seemed quite insecure with math vocabulary and instructions and often asked for clarification of words, questions, and instructions.

Carolyn did not show the presence of retained reflexes or general coordination delays. She did show immature printing and letter formation.

Using the Continuum to determine
a course of action for Carolyn

Carolyn can begin at the processing skills level. She has many challenges around visual processing skills, which can be addressed at this level on the continuum. Math is very logical and orderly. Carolyn will do better with math remediation if her visual memory skills, ability to perceive visual organization, and ability to reason with visual information are improved first.

Amy – Age 16
Background and Testing

Amy is in a special class at school and is making very little progress. Her mom is concerned about her very poor processing skills, weak auditory processing, illegible handwriting, and poor short and long-term memory. Amy has difficulty socially and in all academic areas, even though she really tries. She takes medication for ADHD and depression.

Testing showed that Amy has retained reflexes and core learning skills delays. She showed average visual memory but weak overall processing skills, with auditory skills being particularly weak.

How will these challenges affect Amy's learning?

- Our cognitive processing skills help us understand our world. Weak processing skills will affect all areas of learning and can cause Amy to feel insecure and anxious.
- Amy has done a good job of presenting herself as a "pretty together" girl, in spite of the fact that her listening and processing skills are not supporting her well. This may mask some of her challenges or cause those working with her to misunderstand or not fully recognize her needs.
- Amy's core learning skills delays, slow processing speed, and difficulties with auditory and visual processing make it difficult for her to get complete and accurate information to work with. This may cause her to be afraid she will do things wrong and therefore not initiate conversations or activities. She may also act or sound vague because she feels "lost."

Using the Continuum to determine a course of action for Amy

Because of the number of challenges that Amy is experiencing, she will most likely need training in several segments of the continuum. Her program should begin with Core Learning Skills Training and auditory stimulation. These will improve her listening and attention skills and will help her to feel more aware, comfortable, and in control. Confidence and social skills will likely improve as a result.

Processing skills development should follow Core Learning Skills and auditory training. With this foundation, Amy should be ready to successfully take on reading, math, spelling, and written language remediation. Executive function skills can be developed along with the processing and academic remediation segments.

When children and teens are struggling in school, it is so tempting to attack the academic areas that are showing the low grades. If we look at the number of students who spend years in special education or tutoring programs with little progress toward real independence, it is evident that academic remediation is often too high on the learning skills continuum to be an effective starting place. Students do not always need to start at the bottom or the beginning of the continuum, but it is important to recognize that success at the higher levels is supported by lower-level skills.

Action items. . .
- Go to www.LearningDisability.com.
  Under "Free Articles," read:
    * "A New Look at Learning Challenges Leads to Real Solutions."
- Go to www.FixLearningSkills.com.
    * Listen to "The Learning Skills Continuum."

———————————————— • ————————————————

CHAPTER 8

Core Learning Skills

*How primitive survival reflexes could be getting in the way
of your child developing the visual and motor skills needed
for paying attention and easy learning*

In this chapter. . .

- The role of primitive reflexes in babies
- The signs and symptoms that indicate primitive reflexes from birth and the first months of life are still active
- The typical risk factors for neuro-developmental delay
- Five primitive reflexes that can affect learning
- What skills should be present for a child entering kindergarten?

Identifying and resolving early development problems

Will's story

Night terrors frequently cause ten-year-old Will to run out of his room screaming at night. Will also struggles in school and is a real puzzle and frustration to his parents. He is an overly friendly boy, whom you can't help but like. He is gullible and easily led to do what other people say, even if it is something he knows is bad and would never choose to do without prompting.

Will has trouble walking on a curb. When he throws a ball, his movements are jerky. He throws too hard and too abruptly, so the ball is more likely to smack the person he's playing with than be caught. Will is much too speedy and impulsive. When told to slow down, throw softly, or pay attention, he thinks that he does, but he really makes no change at all.

Will is very eager to please, so at school and on homework, he gets started right away, but after fifteen to twenty minutes of working on something and doing it correctly, he suddenly begins making what seem like ridiculous mistakes. Two plus two becomes five and **l-o-g** spells spin. What's going on? Is he acting up to get attention? Is this his way of getting out of work he doesn't want to do? Could Will do better if he paid closer attention or tried harder?

No! Will *is* trying really hard. In fact, so much energy is going into trying to listen, or play ball, or do the homework that he runs out of steam and fatigues to the point that nothing makes sense anymore. Will doesn't deliberately throw the ball too hard and so abruptly that it hits people. And he isn't gullible and easily pushed to make poor choices because he'll do anything to fit in.

Will is struggling because he has reflexes retained from infancy that are triggering movement patterns that are out of his control. This causes constant neurological interference to body control, attention, and learning, so Will, like most people with retained reflexes, has learned to compensate. He compensates by keeping his body very tense and rigid. This makes some of his movements jerky, but at least he can feel like he's in control.

Being extra-extra friendly is also a compensation—not a conscious one, probably—but one that may allow people to overlook his inconsistent performance and seemingly off-the-wall answers. Even though Will understands right and wrong and is a very good boy, he's too lost in the world to quickly make a decision to say no when someone tells him to do something.

Will looks like a cute, "regular" 4th grade boy, but in reality, he's working so hard to maintain control that after a short period of time his stamina is gone. That's when he becomes wiggly and impulsive and it seems like everything he knows just became disconnected.

Will is one of those kids who confuses his parents and teachers because he has compensated well enough to develop some higher learning skills. He can read, write, and do math. But the strong underlying framework of internal organization, motor, visual, and auditory processing skills that those academics should be standing on, is a shaky, insecure foundation. This makes it look like he just quits trying and quits paying attention. The truth is that when fatigue sets in, the foundation falls apart, and Will can no longer organize and access what he knows.

Will is so used to trying to maintain control by keeping his body tense that he doesn't know how to relax. When his neck finally relaxes as he falls asleep at night, his retained Moro reflex, or "startle" reflex, very likely triggers, throwing him, even in an unconscious state, into "fight or flight," quite possibly the root of his night terrors.

Jimmy's story

Frazzled has become a way of life for Jimmy's mom. She is at her wit's end with her smart little boy, who won't write neatly and is already way behind in school.

Jimmy is a little bundle of energy, with arms and legs flying everywhere and a voice that's usually too speedy, too sassy, and too loud. At seven years old, he has already pegged himself as a "bad boy," so his usual comeback to direction is, "What if I don't?"

What we know from working with Jimmy is that he really does want to succeed. He wants to do a good job and make his teachers and his mom proud. But he has so little control of his body, and he's so absolutely confused by letters and letter sounds that he can't begin to perform as expected. Jimmy cannot get his arms and legs in control to execute the movements he's supposed to. When he tries to copy letters, the result looks like a three-year-old's scribble. He can't pay attention because his body always wants to wiggle around.

So Jimmy takes on a bad attitude to go along with what looks like his "bad behavior." He gives wrong answers to questions he knows; he talks back to his mom and sometimes his teacher; and he runs around recklessly, making lots of noise. "Being bad" is Jimmy's compensation strategy, his way of getting control in a body and a world of reading and writing that are completely out of his control.

Primitive reflexes

Have you ever seen a startled baby fling its arms, legs, and head back; or felt the tight grasp of tiny fingers holding yours? These are primitive reflex behaviors. They are automatic movements, or movements that occur without thought. They originate in the brainstem as opposed to the higher thinking part of the brain.

Primitive survival reflexes are nature's way of providing protection for the fetus in utero and the newborn outside the womb, until higher levels of mental and muscle control can take over. These automatic movements help in the birthing process and with the baby's adjustment to the "outside world."

Movement is the foundation for attention, understanding, and learning. Primitive survival reflexes jump-start learning by triggering involuntary movements. These random movements help the muscles develop the tone, or resting tension, that they need to be ready for action.

As the brain develops, reflex movements lead to trial and error movements, followed by intentional movements. In this process, the primitive reflexes should become integrated or inactive. They are no longer needed because higher levels of the brain are taking control, and the reflexes would simply cause interference to the developing motor and cognitive skills.

As movements are repeated over and over, they become automatic, not needing conscious thought. Ultimately, understanding and control of movement leads to intellectual control, where "movement" and learning occur through visualization, creativity, and mental manipulation, or thinking.

What happens if primitive reflexes do not become inactive when they should?

Primitive reflexes should integrate, or become inactive, within the first twelve months of life. The repetitive movements that babies make help integrate the involuntary reflex movements and pave the way for more specific and sophisticated levels of learning. Typical infant behaviors such as rolling, creeping, and crawling influence the voluntary control of bowel and bladder functions. They are also early stepping stones in the development of skills that children eventually need for school, such as sitting still in a chair and moving the eyes smoothly across a page of text.

A baby turning its head and looking at its hand reaching out is experiencing the very beginning of eye-hand coordination. If primitive reflexes do not integrate or become inactive when they should, these involuntary movements cause the new motor patterns the infant is experiencing to become confused, instead of becoming the automatic learned skills that are the building blocks of higher motor and mental control.

Comfortable, efficient learning rests on a foundation of basic physical skills, such as balance and the coordination of the upper and lower and right and left sides of the body. Retained reflexes can interfere with the development of physical skills, which creates an unstable foundation.

Retained reflexes can also get in the way of the child developing internal organization: understanding where his body is in space, having a sense of left and right and up and down on himself, and internally knowing what to expect from his movements. Seeing the difference between similar letters (b / d); understanding time and space; planning; and organizing his things, homework, and projects are all based on internal skills.

Primitive reflexes are very important in the earliest stages of a child developing physical and visual skills and internal organization. These reflexes should appear and then disappear in a certain order and should last for only a specific amount of time. Many learning and visual problems go back to primitive reflexes that have lingered and outlasted their usefulness.

People are adaptable creatures, so in spite of the interference, they will generally learn to compensate. Sometimes, as in Will's case, the compensations allow higher levels of learning to occur, but have serious consequences when it comes to attention, stamina, and consistency. In Jimmy's case, body control, academics, and attention are so impacted that Jimmy's recourse is to cover his challenges with attitude.

When a student is struggling in school, it may be hard to imagine that working on specific movements to help get primitive reflexes integrated would be a good use of time. Take Max, for example. Max was an 8th grade student who scored well above average on state standardized tests but had very poor performance in school. He had extremely low energy in his voice and body and very poor posture. It seemed like such an effort to do anything other than play his handheld video game, and at thirteen, Max just wasn't very inclined to put out the energy.

Max had primitive reflexes that were still active. He had awkward body movements and little awareness and control of what his limbs were doing. He had learned to compensate by adapting an attitude of not caring and a presentation of slumping and dragging. This made his lack of control and awkwardness look more like "teenage attitude." Max did not do this consciously, but as humans, we do what we need to do to adapt and survive in our world.

When we first began doing the movement activities that would correct the problem and build the underlying skills Max needed, he couldn't see why we were wasting his time with these "stupid, pointless exercises."

Max's instructor explained to him that living with primitive reflexes was like driving a car with a flat tire. You only have a certain amount of fuel in the gas tank. If you're driving with a flat tire, you're going to have to use a lot more fuel to get where you want to go. When Max understood that his lack of body control was using up his fuel, leaving only limited resources for socializing and school, he agreed to get serious about the movement exercises.

Within the first few weeks, Max began to make changes. He was able to stand up taller and had more energy in his body, eyes, and voice. He started to appear more interested and connected, which caused others to want to be around him. As he was able to quit fighting to keep his body in control, he was able to pay better attention in class, and homework did not feel so overwhelming and unmanageable. Max's grades went up, and he gradually was able to shed the apathetic attitude he had used to hide behind.

When primitive reflexes are retained, they can cause neurological interference that affects motor control, sensory perception, visual skills, eye-hand coordination, and thinking. This produces anxiety and causes the person to have to work too hard and with less efficiency than would be expected. This is called neurodevelopmental delay (NDD). Lawrence J. Beuret, M.D., of Palatine, Illinois has developed an NDD Checklist, which includes these risk factors for neurodevelopmental delay:

Pregnancy and Birth:
- Complications with pregnancy, labor, or delivery
- Low birth weight (less than five pounds)
- Delivery more than two weeks early or late
- Difficulties for infant at birth: blue baby, difficulties breathing, heavily bruised, low Apgar scores, distorted skull, jaundice

Infancy:
- Feeding problems in the first six months
- Walking or talking began after eighteen months
- Unusual/severe reactions to immunization
- Illness involving high fever, delirium, convulsions during the first eighteen months

Family History:
- Reading/writing difficulties
- Learning disorders
- Motion sickness
- Underachievers

Learning challenges can be related to neurodevelopmental delay.
Rosemary Boon of Learning Discoveries Psychological Services in NSW, Australia has compiled the following list of challenges related to neurodevelopmental delay.

- Dyslexia or learning difficulties, especially reading, spelling, and comprehension
- Poor written expression
- Poor sequencing skills
- Poor sense of time
- Poor visual function/processing skills
- Slow in processing information
- Attention and concentration problems
- Inability to sit still/fidgeting

- Poor organizational skills
- Easily distracted and/or impulsive
- Hyperactivity
- Hypersensitivity to sound, light, or touch
- Dyspraxia/speech problems and language delays
- Motor, coordination, and balance problems
- Poor posture and/or awkward gait
- Poor handwriting
- Poor spatial awareness
- Poor eye-hand coordination
- Poor gross and fine motor skills
- Difficulty learning how to swim/ride a bike
- Clumsiness/accident prone
- Slow at copying tasks
- Confusion between right and left
- Reversals of letters/numbers and midline problems
- Quick temper/easily frustrated/short fuse
- Bedwetting past five years of age
- Can't cope with change/must have things a certain (their) way
- School phobia
- Poor motivation and/or self-esteem
- Depression, anxiety, or stress
- Behavioral, self-esteem, and motivational problems associated with the above
- In adults, symptoms include agoraphobia (fear of leaving a safe environment such as the home), excessive reaction to stimuli, anxiety, panic attacks, difficulty making decisions, and poor self-esteem.

Five primitive reflexes that are suspect in learning problems

There are five primitive reflexes that seem to have particularly strong consequences for learning.

The Moro Reflex occurs at nine weeks in utero and should disappear when the baby is two to four months old. The Moro Reflex is the startle reflex. It is an involuntary response to threat or sudden change. The baby's head and legs extend and its arms push out away from its body.

When a child retains the Moro reflex, he may become hyper-sensitive to light and sound. He will have trouble paying attention because his eyes are drawn to every change in light or movement in the environment, and his ears are picking up too much infor-mation, causing him to feel overloaded.

When the Moro reflex continues to be active after it should, the child may operate in a fairly constant state of fight or flight. This leads to fatigue, mood swings, and poor ability to adapt. The child may be wary, fearful, or anxious, at least beneath the surface, and carry herself rigidly.

The hyper-alert state of fight or flight causes the body to contin-ually produce the stress hormones adrenaline and cortisol. When these hormones are in constant use in the child's life, they are diverted from their primary function, which is to support the im-mune system. As a result, these children are prone to allergies, ear and throat infections, and chemical and nutritional imbalances.

When the Moro reflex is retained, it contributes to inner ear and vestibular problems, such as poor balance and coordination and poor control of eye movements, which may cause problems with information processing.

The **Tonic Labyrinthine Reflex** or TLR occurs at sixteen weeks in utero and should integrate at approximately four months of age. When the baby's head goes forward, his legs and arms bend and come in toward his body. When the head goes back, the baby's arms and legs straighten. This reflex helps the new-born straighten out at birth and begins to train balance, muscle tone, and proprioception, or the ability to know the position of different body parts.

If this reflex does not integrate when it should, it gets in the way of developing gravitational security. The child may literally and figuratively feel a little off-balance much of the time because his center of balance is thrown off every time his head moves. He doesn't develop a strong sense of himself as the reference point from which to view the world. He never gets a secure sense of where he is in space, which can affect his sense of direction and understanding of up/down, left/right, and front/back. Interestingly, astronauts in a gravity-free environment (where there is no secure reference point) will show some of the same symptoms that learners with poor reference point do: writing from right to left, reversing letters and numbers, and producing mirror writing.

The **Spinal Galant** reflex occurs at twenty weeks in utero and integrates at nine months of age. When the baby's skin is touched on either side of the lower spine, the hips will flex towards that side. This reflex helps with the birthing process and allows the fetus to hear and feel vibration in utero by pushing its spine up against the mother's.

If it is retained beyond nine months, the Spinal Galant can interfere with bladder control, causing bedwetting beyond age five. Children with this reflex don't like tight fitting clothing around their waist, and when they have to sit in a chair, they are likely to fidget and squirm and wiggle. It is very difficult to sit still when you have a reflex causing your hips to flex every time you lean against the back of your chair. This reflex is always competing with the child's attention and short-term memory because the child is distracted by the need to be in a constant state of motion.

The **Asymmetrical Tonic Neck Reflex** or ATNR occurs at eighteen weeks in utero and integrates at six months of age. When the baby's head turns, its arm and leg will extend on the same side. In utero, this reflex helps the fetus move its head from side to side, swing its arms, and kick its legs. These movements help develop muscle tone (strength and readiness to move) and the vestibular system (sense of balance and movement) which is housed in the inner ear. It helps the infant get its first understanding of coordinating both sides of the body to work together. This is needed later for crawling, walking, and skipping with coordinated interweaving movements. An important function of the ATNR is to train the baby's eyes. It is the very beginning of eye-hand coordination, which is later needed for eating, writing, throwing, or any coordinated movement that uses the hand and eyes together.

By six months of age, the ATNR is no longer needed, and further developed movement patterns should be coming in to replace it. If it is retained, it can cause problems with balance, mental and physical confusion with the relationship of the two sides of the body, difficulty with distance vision, and problems with eye-hand coordination. A child with this reflex may walk with the same arm and leg moving forward instead of using the opposite arm and leg, making him look like a robot. This awkwardness will make sports difficult and will set the child up as a target for teasing.

Retention of this reflex can get in the way of reading, spelling, and writing fluency. The child may have difficulty with handwriting and holding a pencil. She will tend to hold the pencil too loosely, or may compensate by holding it too tightly, which is very tiring.

The **Symmetrical Tonic Neck Reflex** occurs at six to nine months of age and should integrate by nine to eleven months. This reflex helps the infant learn to rise on hands and knees in order to creep and crawl. Creeping and crawling are essential for visual development. In fact, creeping is one of most important movement patterns for helping the eyes move across the midline (vertical center line) of the body. As the infant moves from one hand to another, the eyes also move from one side to the other. This is very important training for reading. Without the ability to move the eyes easily across midline, the child will lose his place often when reading, and lose his attention as he crosses the page when writing.

The Kindergartener as a finely-tuned organism

When Sally bounces into her kindergarten class on her first day of school, she is bringing with her a remarkable set of skills, or at least it is assumed that she is. These are skills that have been developing since the onset of movement in the womb. They are fed by all of the senses and are becoming more and more sophisticated as the developing brain is able to orchestrate more complex movements. Children coming into a traditional kindergarten class must already have developed the attention and body control to do such things as:

- Sit on the rug and look at the teacher without bumping other children. This requires balance; a sense of space; ability to control the arms, legs, posture, and head; and the ability to look and listen without getting distracted.

- Look at the exact spot the teacher is pointing to on the calendar and follow her finger as she moves across the days so the children can count. This requires the eyes to look at things at a distance, move from one spot to another accurately and stop there, and follow a target (the teacher's finger) smoothly.

- Drive a tricycle around on the playground without crashing or veering off the sidewalk road. The eyes must be the steering wheel, looking ahead to where the child is going, as well as noticing the surrounding environment. The two sides of the body must work together in a coordinated rhythm. The child must be able to judge distance and space, and feel secure, with a good sense of balance.

- Clap rhythms and play hand games with other children. This requires a sense of timing, the ability to put together movement with what is seen and heard, and a sense of pressure that helps the children judge if they are clapping or "high fiving" too hard or too softly.

- Recognize letters and numbers. This requires a sense of left and right, up and down; attention to fine visual detail; and eyes that can focus together on a stimulus.

All of these skills and many, many more are needed for success in kindergarten. The demands for body and attention awareness and control; visual control; sense of space and time; and refined, controlled movements increase with each grade level. Delays in early development will impact attention, body control, and thinking at higher levels, making it difficult for the student to comfortably manage the expectations of the classroom and playground.

When students come in our door with learning or attention challenges, we know that we cannot look at the symptoms in isolation. We have to look at how the whole body and all the sensory systems are working together. This includes the vestibular system, the key system for sense of balance and response to gravity, and the proprioceptive system, our sense of pressure and where the body parts are in space.

If primitive reflexes are retained or any of the key sensory systems for learning—auditory, visual, vestibular, proprioceptive, or touch—are delayed, other systems will have to work overtime, causing everything to be harder than it should be. Addressing these neurodevelopmental delays will be critical to the process of correcting a person's learning and attention challenges.

Action items. . .
- Go to www.LearningDisability.com.
  Under "Free Articles," read:
    * "Lazy Is NOT a Diagnosis."
- Go to www.FixLearningSkills.com.
    * Listen to "Why Does My Kid Act That Way?"

CHAPTER 9

Attention and Memory Q&A

Why are attention and memory so foundational to learning?

In this chapter. . .
- Three essential types of attention
- How poor memory and attention skills sabotage learning
- Why children can have great attention for video games but poor attention for homework
- Why medication is not the right answer for many children

All learning depends on these two basics.

Attention and memory are bottom line learning skills. They are like the brain's receptionist for information. If a child can't focus long enough to let the information in, or if he doesn't have a way to hold on to it, there will be interference to all further learning. G. Reid Lyon, formerly of the National Institute of Mental Health, said, "Human learning and behavior are dependent upon the ability to:

- Pay attention to the critical features in the environment;
- Retain and retrieve information; and
- Select, deploy, monitor, and control cognitive strategies to learn, remember, and think."[1]

In other words, learning and behavior depend upon attention, memory, and executive function, the brain's decision-making function. These learning skills are also highly dependent upon each other. In this chapter, we will focus on two factors – memory and attention. We will take a look at executive function in Chapter 11.

How do poor attention skills affect memory?

Stephen has a good memory. He's pretty confident that when someone gives him directions, he'll be able to get there because he can easily picture the route in his mind. Stephen doesn't have great attention skills, however. While a friend was giving him directions to the party he was planning to attend that evening, his attention was drifting in and out.

As he's driving to the party, Stephen realizes that he can't remember the street name or which way he is supposed to turn. As a result of his inefficient attention, Stephen only got part of the message. Even with good memory skills, it's hard to remember information that is spotty or confusing.

How is attention affected when the memory span cannot support the amount of information coming in?

Sandi has good attention skills but her memory span is weak. By 5th grade, students should be able to take in and hold onto six or more pieces of information, so if her teacher is lecturing in phrases of five to seven words, a 5th grader should be able to keep up. Sandi, however, can only take-in four pieces of information at a time. Every time her brain takes a split second to grasp the information coming in, she misses a word or two that the teacher says because her chunks of information have up to four words, and the teacher's phrases are typically longer than that. Pretty soon, Sandi finds her attention drifting because what she's hearing isn't making sense.

Sandi's class has just had a lecture on the Revolutionary War. Here's what the teacher said, "The Redcoats tried to do everything by the book in the traditional ways. They lined up their troops and marched into battle the way a marching band marches down the street. This made them vulnerable to the rebels who were hiding in the trees ready to fire on the masses of British troops." Here's what Sandi heard, "The Redcoats tried to…book in traditional ways… and marched into battle…down the street. This made them…hide in the trees…of British troops."

The class is ready for their discussion of the material. When the teacher asks, "What was the British method of fighting a battle?"

Sandi raises her hand and says, "They used a book and hid in trees." Everyone laughs. The teacher tells Sandi to pay attention. Sandi feels stupid, and after awhile, quits contributing during discussions.

Can attention or memory problems ever be the symptom but not the problem?

Memory and attention problems can actually be symptoms of other learning skills challenges. Rick has poor listening skills. He doesn't realize that the teacher's voice doesn't sound muted and garbled to anyone else, so he never mentions it. He just works extremely hard to get the information.

By the middle of the period, he's exhausted, and he finds that he has started to daydream. The teacher said something about a test or a quiz on Tuesday, or was it Thursday? Well, it was one day next week; he can't remember. Rick can't remember because he did not get complete and accurate information. He began to daydream because his attention was so stressed by having to work so hard to listen that he couldn't maintain it.

What are the three types of attention needed for learning?

There are three types of attention that greatly impact learning: sustained attention, selective attention, and divided attention. Five-year-old Sammy has appropriate *sustained attention* for his age. He can keep his attention on the colorful storybook the teacher is reading to the class, all the way to the end of the story. Rachel, sitting next to him, starts wiggling and looking around during the story. She pokes Sammy and tries to tell him something. She notices the story again but pretty soon is twisting around to see what's happening outside. Rachel has a very short attention span, or *sustained attention.*

Carly has good *selective attention* skills. In spite of distractions, she can keep herself focused on task. Today is lawn maintenance day at school, so it's loud outside and warm and stuffy inside with the doors closed. She notices these things but is able to choose to finish her reading and questions.

Her friend Kelsey, on the other hand, hates lawn day. She can't block the noise, and it's making it hard to think. And she's so uncomfortable in this stuffy classroom. If she'd only worn a t-shirt instead of a sweater today maybe she wouldn't be so hot and she could concentrate better.

Divided attention is a high-level-thinking skill. It allows us to pay attention to more than one thing at a time, even as new information is coming in. Moms everywhere use this skill as they manage to answer their three-year-old's multitude of questions, put groceries from their list in the shopping cart, and mentally calculate what the total bill will be. Jason uses divided attention to take notes in class. He has to pay attention to what the teacher is saying, mentally extract the key ideas, and put them on paper in an organized fashion while the teacher is continuing to talk.

Students with weak divided attention skills will have trouble taking notes because they get stuck focusing on one part of the process and miss information. They may end up with good notes for a few pieces of the lecture but few notes for the rest, or a full page of notes taken throughout the lecture that don't make any sense. These students can't listen, organize, think, and write all at the same time because one or more pieces of the process demands too much of their attention.

Why is my child so impulsive?

Impulsiveness is usually associated with attention problems, but can also be a symptom of memory challenges. Evan is extremely impulsive. He has good things to say and blurts them out as soon as they come into his mind. He also has to be first all the time, so he races in front of people and impulsively pushes them out of the way. Evan doesn't want to be annoying but can't seem to stop himself. In fact, he's not usually even aware that he's being impulsive. This is an attention problem related to self-regulation.

Chaz is also impulsive, but he says things as soon as they come to mind because he's so afraid he'll forget if he doesn't get it out right now. Chaz can be impulsive in his actions for the same reason. He remembers that his mom gave him a note to give to the teacher, and he jumps up to get it and give it to her, even though the teacher is in the middle of a lesson. If he doesn't do it right now, he knows he'll forget for sure.

Karen looks impulsive, but she's really not. Karen has very slow response time. She needs time to process the question asked and come up with a response, so she says anything that comes to mind just to fill in the gap while she thinks.

Why can my child play video games for hours but can't sit and do homework for five minutes?

Children with attention challenges can be very frustrating to parents because they can pay attention to things they are interested in but are "bored" and yawning the second they start their homework. I can't begin to count the number of times I've heard parents tell me that their child is the best on the block at video games, but can drag a fifteen-minute homework assignment out into an hour because he can't keep his attention on it.

First of all, it's important to recognize the difference in intensity level between video games and homework. Video games are highly stimulating and constantly changing, so what looks like sustained attention, isn't. Also, things that interest us automatically trigger a higher level of attention, so it is very natural for children to attend better to things they are especially interested in. What's challenging for students with attention deficits is that to focus on something they are not as interested in takes much more energy and attention than average, and this is hard to sustain.

Is medication the right answer if my child has an attention problem?

Medication should never be the *first* answer and is often not the *right* answer to an attention problem. When a child is struggling with school or grades, accompanied by an attention problem, it is important first to determine if attention is the cause of the school struggles, or merely a symptom of something else not working right.

Retained primitive reflexes, weak memory skills, or delays in any area of processing or executive function can make paying attention difficult, if not impossible. Nutritional or biochemical imbalances can be the root of poor behavior and attention. Medication may possibly cover the symptoms, but it will not fix neurodevelopmental learning skills delays and will not teach a child to read.

Is there ever a time when medication is appropriate? Perhaps, but with far, far less frequency than is currently the standard. Prescription drug commercials on television would have us believe that drugs are the answer to almost anything. After all, who wouldn't want to be like that vibrant, happy young couple galloping down the beach on a beautiful white horse laughing, the wind blowing their hair just the right amount? But listen closely. Every single one of those purportedly marvelous life-changing drugs comes with its own nightmare list of possible side affects.

About 3–5 percent of school-age children go to school everyday having taken their Ritalin, a cocaine-based medication. Even preschoolers, children in the two- to five-year-old age range, are now taking this very powerful drug. In the *Physician's Desk Reference* (PDR), Ritalin has a list of twenty-five side effects including anxiety, weight loss, hair loss, nausea, headaches, and interruption of growth.

Attention Deficit Hyperactivity Disorder (ADHD) is typically treated with stimulant medications such as Ritalin, Dexadrine, Adderall, And Cylert. If these don't work, anti-depressants, such as Prozac or Wellbutrin might be used. Antihypertensives and antipsychotics are sometimes prescribed in ADHD treatment. Make no mistake, these are powerful drugs, and they will affect brain chemistry.

Medical pioneer in the field of brain imaging and attention, Daniel Amen, M.D., recognizes that dietary interventions, intense aerobic exercise, nutritional supplements, and training are an important part of the treatment for attention problems.[2] In addition, before prescribing medication, he may recommend doing a SPECT Study[3] (brain scan) to actually look at the brain to see what's really happening. The brain is the only organ in the body that is typically treated medically without looking at it to see what's going on.

I have seen a few (the operative words here being *a few*) children who have been helped dramatically with medication, and I recognize that there is sometimes a place for it. But it should come as a last resort and always be used as a part of a whole treatment plan. Organization and routine at home, nutritional guidance to control food allergies and sensitivities, exercise, and attention skills training are all first steps and highly effective, particularly when used in conjunction with each other.

Can attention skills really be improved?

Attention skills can be increased through specific and intensive training. Even if the child is on a special diet, nutritional supplements, or medication, he still needs to learn how to control his attention. If people are going to do more than just manage symptoms, they must become aware of what it feels like to pay attention and what it feels like when they're not. They must recognize their losses of attention and have strategies to regain their focus.

Attention awareness and control can be built through training, as well as increasing sustained, selective, and divided attention. We will specifically address attention training in Chapter 18. The important thing to know here is that attention skills can be improved and absolutely should be. Otherwise, the child's family life, school performance, social relationships, and future will be ruled by his attention deficit.

Is memory selective? Why can my child remember certain things really well but not remember his times tables or directions I give him?

Andy can remember the statistics for all his favorite pro baseball players, but he can't remember the three things his dad just told him to do. Andy has probably read and recited the stats on his baseball cards over and over. This information has made it to his long-term memory.

Long-term memory relies on information being experienced repeatedly to the point that a neuronal change has occurred in the brain—a lasting connection has been made. The things that make it to long-term memory get there by way of practice and rehearsal or as the result of a unique or impacting experience. Everyone born before about 1995 will remember where they were on the morning of September 11, 2001.

Memory is a composite of three functions: short-term memory, working memory, and long-term memory. Short-term memory is not permanent memory. It is the gateway for information coming in, but is actually a temporary electrical trace that will only last for a matter of seconds.

Working memory, like short-term memory, is not permanent but is an active holding room for information while we are using it or thinking about it. A rehearsal strategy, such as hearing it again in our mind or visualizing it, allows the working memory to hang onto and manipulate the information. Previous knowledge from long-term memory may help determine how to think about or act upon the incoming data.

The directions that Andy's dad quickly rattled off went into Andy's short-term memory. If Andy is going to remember and follow through with what his father told him to do, he will hear what his dad said, then hear it again and/or visualize it in his mind. As he goes through the process of following those instructions, he will likely continue to mentally "hear" or visualize them, allowing him to remember long enough to follow through. In the absence of good listening, attention, or memory strategies, the instructions will be forgotten.

Memory is aided greatly by comprehension and association. Many students try to remember information such as spelling words and math facts by rote as random, non-meaningful pieces of information. This is very difficult and will have very limited success. When students don't really understand math concepts and how numbers work, they will typically have trouble remembering math facts. They have no way to think about them or associate them, so they are using a completely rote approach.

The same is true with spelling. When students have difficulty processing the sounds and syllables in words, they will try to remember the spelling of words without any reference point for the order or number of sounds and syllables that should be in them.

Many people have difficulty remembering names of people they just met. The name comes into short-term memory as a basically random piece of information. Unless the person makes a conscious effort to rehearse or associate the name in some way, it will dissipate as the brief electrical trace that it is.

Short term and working memory are intended to help gather information and work with it in the present. This is the starting point for establishing a data bank in the brain. The cells are alerted to new information and begin to form a chain for processing it. The more frequently the cells are activated with the same information, the more they will begin to record the information and retain it.

Two critical factors in short-term memory are quantity and quality. If the input the brain is getting is confusing because of poor attention, listening skills, or visual processing, the *quality* of the information will be compromised, and it is not likely to make it to long-term memory. *Quantity* refers to the number of digits, or pieces of information (such as letters, numbers, or words), that people can take-in in one chunk. The average digit span for children eight-and-a-half years old is five to six digits. Adults can usually hold seven and sometimes as many as nine digits.

Note that children are now expected to begin reading at five and six years old. Their memory capacity is usually about three to four digits at that age, but their reading and spelling words (such as *yellow* and *something*) may have as many as six to eight letters. Children with a low or even average digit span who try to memorize their multi-syllable spelling and vocabulary words by rote, without the benefit of understanding how to chunk words into syllables and sounds, will experience frustration and failure.

Can memory skills really be increased?

Through specific training, memory skills can be increased. The use of inner language is an important factor in building and using memory. When someone tells you a phone number that you are going to dial right away, you will most likely say the number to yourself over and over in your mind until you have dialed it. This is using auditory inner language. If you can't write the number down, but you need to remember it for later, you will probably also visualize the numbers. This is using your visual inner language. Use of inner language is an integral part of memory, comprehension, executive function, and learning in general.

Once a child's memory span has been increased, it will be important to teach all of the skills that were missed because they relied on a memory that was immature. For example, in reading, if the student could not recall the letter symbols when reading was being taught, then the skills of sounding out words, scanning for key words, alphabetizing, and spelling all have been missed because they are taught rapidly with the early reading experiences. We cannot assume that the gaps will automatically fill in just because the memory capacity is now available.

Attention and memory are the gateway, filter, and storage centers for information. They are critical components of every aspect of learning and are highly involved with executive function in guiding one's actions and movement toward independence.

Action items. . .
- Go to www.LearningDisability.com.
  Under "Free Articles," read:
    * "Attention Focus Challenges."
    * "Why Can't They Remember?"
- Go to www.FixLearningSkills.com.
    * Listen to "Memory and Attention Issues."

—————————————————————————— • ——————

CHAPTER 10

Auditory Processing

Are your child's struggles the result of poor listening skills?

In this chapter. . .

- The ability to listen and process sounds properly is critical to learning
- Poor auditory processing can mask as other difficulties
- Understanding listening development in order to identify and treat auditory processing problems in the correct sequence
- The many and varied behaviors and challenges that can be related to an auditory processing problem
- The role of physiology and intention in listening

Listening skills are foundational to success in life.

Poor listening has long been blamed when spouses argue or misunderstand each other, when children don't follow directions at school or ignore their parents, or when communication breaks down in the workplace. However, it is rarely taken seriously as an actual and *unintentional* cause for these problems. Listening plays an enormous role in relationships, communication, learning, well-being, and overall functioning. In spite of that fact, auditory processing (listening and how we think about information that we hear) has been grossly overlooked and underestimated in its importance for living a quality life.

Traditionally, if children have movement problems, we give them movement therapy. If they have speech problems we give them speech therapy. Reading, writing, and spelling problems are given academic therapy. Individuals with behavior and social problems are given counseling. Attention challenges are often addressed with medication, although we don't generally recommend the use of drugs with our students. (This is a great comfort to many parents who are concerned about the possible long-term consequences of their children taking prescriptions.)

When these therapies appear targeted but not productive enough, there may be something underlying that is keeping the individual from making the expected connections and changes. The key may be an under-active auditory system.

Auditory processing challenges are a primary factor in the learning difficulties experienced by our students today. The relationship and communication problems that are rampant in our society can be linked to poorly developed listening skills.

What do these symptoms have in common?

- Lack of engagement
- Mispronouncing sounds and words
- Getting lost in conversation
- Poor social skills
- Trouble with language, learning, and communication
- Low energy and coordination
- Reading problems
- Messy handwriting
- Difficulty with organization
- Attention problems

What do all of these things have in common? They are all connected with auditory processing, with listening.

Strong assets undermined by weak listening skills

Kathy was a gifted 6th grader. Gifted and dyslexic. She had extremely weak phonemic awareness (the auditory processing skill needed to think about the sounds in words) and struggled with reading, writing, and expressive language. She had a strong visual-spatial thinking style which allowed her to mentally picture things from all different angles, but it also caused her to have confusion about symbols (letters, words, and punctuation marks) and feel disoriented when she looked at the page. Not only could she <u>not</u> sound out words, but she reported, "The words seem to wiggle around and run off the page when I try to read them."

Because visual-spatial thinkers are very global in their thought processes and can rapidly think about many different things at one time, language, which is sequential and fairly slow in comparison, can be challenging, both to listen to and to express.

Kathy had excellent logic and reasoning skills and a very supportive mom. It frustrated her that she had to have help from her mom, and she had become quite angry about it, making things a bit tough at home. Kathy was outgoing but very self-conscious about her learning challenges. This was affecting her relationships and attitude at school.

Camouflaging the problem

In his fifth grade class, Mike was quiet and compliant. He read fairly well, though he seemed to lack confidence. He always looked like he knew what he was doing in class and never seemed to have any questions. He did take a lot of class work home, but it, along with his homework, always came back correct. Mike was getting pretty good grades, was a nice boy, and was never disruptive or unhappy in class.

Mike was doing a really good job of covering up his struggles by not standing out in class. What his mom saw at home, however, was a different story. He had extreme anxiety about school. Several times a week during the school year, he complained of headaches and stomachaches. Mike brought enormous amounts of unfinished class work home to complete along with his homework. And he needed so much help understanding it that his mom felt like she was going through the 5th grade a second time. His grades were really more reflective of her spoon-feeding him information than of him really getting it.

Mike's comprehension was "black and white" and focused on details while missing the whole. He seemed to have trouble moving information from short-term memory to long-term memory. He tried to remember information by rote without meaning, and as a result, couldn't seem to remember it at all. This not only caused him to struggle with schoolwork, but it affected his social understanding as well. He was very upset by change, and when he went somewhere, such as a restaurant, he didn't seem to connect with what is going on around him. He just didn't see the big picture.

Mike's challenges with comprehension were two-fold. First, he was not grounded and oriented in space. He felt a bit lost most of the time and had difficulty accurately judging what was going on around him. This alone can be very disconcerting. He was not getting clear, accurate input auditorily, so he was always on "high alert," just trying to figure out how to act so he didn't look stupid. As a result, he was very black and white in his thinking and very rigid and disrupted by change. He couldn't process new things quickly enough, so any change would make him feel anxious.

In addition, Mike was not processing sounds in language accurately, so much of what he was hearing didn't really make sense. He knew it should make sense, so he just acted like he knew what was going on. In reality, he was too lost to even know what questions to ask the teacher, so he saved his work to do at home, where his mom could sit with him in a quiet environment and explain things to him more slowly. The one-to-one attention was helpful because he could get clues from watching his mom's mouth and because she recognized when he didn't understand without him having to ask questions.

Auditory Stimulation and Training strengthens listening skills.

Kathy and Mike's difficulties in school were related to weak listening skills and were able to be corrected through Auditory Stimulation and Training. Kathy's reading and spelling were clearly affected by her very weak ability to identify and think about the individual sounds in words, an auditory processing skill called phonemic awareness.

Kathy went through a twenty-week program of auditory stimulation and training, coupled with techniques to help her be aware of and control the disorientation. The auditory stimulation opened avenues in Kathy's learning and self-esteem that allowed her to be comfortable with who she was and blossom academically.

Mike had actually gone through a significant amount of tutoring using good programs and strategies before he began his program of Auditory Stimulation and Training. He had shown some improvements in decoding, spelling, and comprehension, but it wasn't until he started a program to stimulate and train listening skills that things began to come together for him. After two weeks of listening, he was sleeping better, and after five weeks, he had become more outgoing and assertive. He began taking initiative and showing some independence. After seven weeks, Mike was able to summarize much better and was asking many more questions.

Mike took a setback in mid-August in nervous anticipation of the beginning of school, but found that for the first time, he understood the teacher's directions and did not experience anxiety in school. At the end of Mike's twenty-week listening program, his mom said that they were "thrilled with the changes and couldn't believe how fast he was catching on to everything." He was getting good grades on his own, and even Mike said that he felt his listening program had helped. Three months after training, Mike's mom reported that Mike was continuing to do well and that "school is so easy for him now!"

Listening and social skills

Janie is a twenty-four-year-old graduate student. She's cute, she's smart, and she drives her roommate crazy. She talks too loudly and too much. In fact she talks incessantly. And she never listens. If others try to interject something, she usually talks right over them. One of the ways that people get around their poor listening skills is to dominate the conversation. If they can do all the talking, they never have to listen.

D.J. is a very lonely ten-year-old. He is bossy and belligerent, at least in his tone of voice. He speaks too loudly, and his voice has an abrupt abrasive edge to it. Other kids don't like him because he sounds mean. D.J. isn't mean. He has a listening problem. He doesn't really hear how he sounds, so he can't monitor and adjust either his volume or his tone.

Listening skills and language

We met seven-year-old Alita and eleven-year-old Evan in earlier chapters. Both of these children had virtually no language when we met them due to severe auditory processing delays. Karen Foli, writer and parent of a child with an auditory processing disorder, wrote a book entitled *Like Sound Through Water.* [1] This is a good word picture for what it must be like to have a severe auditory processing problem.

I had a student once tell me that for him, listening was like the "wah, wah, wah" that Charles Schulz's character Patti hears when she listens to her teacher in the *Peanuts* cartoons. He said that when he listens to people talk, it often seems like they are talking too fast, and after awhile, it sounds like an electric drill in his head. No wonder he was so anxious and always struggled to comprehend and follow oral directions.

Understanding, learning, and using language depends upon good auditory input. If the message that the language part of the brain receives is unclear or incomplete, confusion with language will occur. Clearing up the auditory processing or listening problem is the first step in improving language comprehension and expression.

Listening and attention

Have you ever sat in a lecture that was way over your head? Pretty soon, you probably found your attention drifting. It is very hard to for people to maintain their attention on something that doesn't make sense to them. Weak auditory processing skills will cause a person to miss information when listening. Even if they are trying really hard to piece it together, it will eventually be too taxing or too confusing to continue paying attention. Listening problems in a classroom or conversation often look just like an attention problem.

At a staff meeting one afternoon, I did an auditory processing simulation for my staff. I didn't tell them that it was a simulation. I just told then that I had a very interesting recording that I wanted them to listen to and take notes on. The recording was actually distorted so that it was intelligible, but just barely. The recording was only ninety seconds long, but the response of various staff members was fascinating.

One very diligently tried to take notes the whole time, in spite of the fact that it wasn't making sense and she was becoming visibly stressed. One slammed her pencil down after about thirty seconds. Another leaned back in her chair and crossed her arms. One young man started poking the person next to him and making jokes. Another started looking around the room to see what everyone else was doing.

The staff's behaviors were classic responses to an auditory processing delay: anxiety and loss of attention.

When I did this same simulation in a professional seminar, one participant broke down in tears and said, "That's my life." Can you imagine the stress that a child with an auditory processing problem goes through day after day, straining to listen and maintain his attention? He is using a phenomenal amount of energy and effort, but to the onlooker, it may look like he's not paying attention.

Listening skills development

The development of listening skills parallels overall human development. The initial stage involves self-awareness. The child explores her own movements and develops increasing control of her muscles and balance. As she starts to know the difference between herself and others, she wants to make connections.

This emerging ego-world understanding is the next major stage in development. It centers around interaction, communication, and relationships. The highest level of development is academic learning, executive function, and higher thinking.

These three stages of human development correlate generally with the brainstem, limbic system (the emotional part of the brain), and the cortex (the higher-thinking part of the brain). When we do Auditory Stimulation and Training to improve listening skills, we follow these levels in order to identify and treat challenges in the appropriate sequence.

We call these levels: FEET, HEART, and HEAD. As we have seen, challenges at lower levels can cause difficulties at higher levels. A reading problem may not just be a HEAD level problem. If there are challenges at the FEET or HEART level, they will interfere with higher learning and must be corrected first.

FEET level challenges

At the FEET level of listening development, the child is gaining information about himself and developing a sense of himself as the reference point from which to view and learn about the world. He is developing those core learning skills that help him internally organize for higher learning and mental control.

These skills include laterality (right and left sidedness), orientation in space, motor skills, coordination of movement, and posture. The auditory and vestibular systems, both of which are housed in the inner ear, are involved with this level of development.

Challenges at the FEET level of listening development will be related to poor orientation in space, motor control, and lack of internal organization. Symptoms include the following types of behaviors:

- Scattered / Not focused
- Rigid / Overwhelmed by change / "Hanging on too tight"
- Bumps into things
- Can't parallel park
- Poor organization on the page
- Poor handwriting
- Clumsy
- Loses things / Never knows where things are such as homework, keys, or driver's license
- Doesn't finish a sentence
- Changes the subject often
- Can't read maps

Gabrielle was a dreamy six-year-old girl who seemed to float through space. She drifted around and never seemed to be able to land and stay in one place. She was, understandably, having difficulty paying attention and learning in school.

On the first day of her listening program, she drew a picture of herself and her family (below). Notice how nothing in her picture is grounded in space. Everything is floating.

Now look at her picture just two weeks later after starting her Samonas Sound Therapy (listening) program. She was more grounded and settled personally, and it showed in her drawing as well.

HEART level challenges

Listening development at the HEART level is about the child gaining information about himself in relation to others and the world. Problems in this area may cause people to have trouble self-monitoring their voice and how they are coming across. A child may sound very defensive or be overly cranky but not realize it because he doesn't hear how he sounds. Sometimes children have behaviors, such as being quirky or bossy or shy that are looked at as personality traits, but are actually the child struggling to adapt to the environment.

HEART level listening challenges affect attention; higher-level orientation and organization in space; and comprehension of language, the environment, and what is happening socially. Symptoms include the following kinds of behaviors:

- Poor attention when listening
- Misses information when listening
- Poor sense of social space
- Doesn't "get" what's going on around her
- Misses social cues
- Doesn't know why people get mad at him
- Makes poor decisions
- Gets lost in conversation
- Creates own reality
- Trouble getting started or completing tasks

Mike, who we met earlier in this chapter, had challenges at the HEART level. He missed information when listening, had difficulty getting started with anything on his own, was quiet and withdrawn, and had great difficulty assessing what was going on around him.

Amy, a junior in high school, had challenges in this area that isolated her socially. She had a brusque way of talking that put people off. She tended to stand too close to people and speak too loudly. Her mom said that other students her age didn't like her because she was "a lot of work."

Amy couldn't carry on a conversation well, so the other person always had to keep things going. She typically shied away from social situations, and her mom was concerned about how reclusive she was.

After starting her Auditory Stimulation and Training program in the summer, Amy began wanting to be social with the family. By the time school started in the fall, she had made so much change in demeanor and communication, both in the words she used and in the intonation and expression of her language, that she made new friends, became active in her youth group at church, and started going out and doing things with friends on weekends.

HEAD level challenges

The highest level of listening development, the HEAD level, involves our higher thinking, learning, organizing, and reasoning. Good listening skills actually provide energy to the cortex, the thinking part of the brain, for motivation and processing all of the fine details of information needed for academic learning, refined social communication, and problem-solving.

Challenges at this level will tend to relate to language, verbal organization, phonemic awareness, task organization and completion, and academics. Symptoms of HEAD level challenges involve such behaviors as:

- "Mishearing" words
- Mispronouncing words
- Trouble organizing thoughts
- Words don't come out right
- Trouble with phonics, reading, spelling
- Avoiding schoolwork
- Working too hard for minimum outcome
- Problems with reading comprehension
- Trouble organizing and planning long term projects
- Difficulty multi-tasking

Kathy, who we met at the beginning of this chapter, was experiencing challenges primarily at this level. She had extremely weak phonemic awareness that was getting in the way of her understanding and learning phonics for reading and spelling. But she also had issues with spatial orientation and language sequencing and expression that had to be dealt with. Her listening protocol focused first on grounding and orientation, then on language expression, and finally on the finer discrimination needed for phonemic awareness, working up from FEET to HEART to HEAD.

The physiology and intention of listening

The shape of the ear, and the fact that we have two of them, triggers our attention and makes us aware of the presence of sound. It also helps us to know where the sound is coming from.

The middle ear is hugely important in both hearing and listening. Its job is to protect the ear, transmit sound, and tune-in and tune-out for listening. The major players here are the tiniest bones and muscles in the body. They have to move the sound from the middle ear, which is like a little air-filled chamber with a door on each end, to the inner ear, which is filled with fluid.

Because it is harder to move sound through liquid than air, a significant amount of power has to be generated by the middle ear muscles and bones in order to create enough pressure to move the message through the inner ear clearly.

This is a critical piece of understanding, in light of the fact that a tremendous number of children have recurrent ear infections during their language development years. Ear infections temporarily weaken the middle ear's ability to move sound effectively to the inner ear because of the fluid that builds up in the middle ear and creates resistance. This distorts the signal causing the listener to get a poor incoming message.

The middle ear muscles are small but mighty! Through continuous communication between the middle ear and the brain, the flexing or constricting of these little muscles helps protect the ear from excessively loud sounds. In addition, they appear to be actively involved with tuning-in to sound. This allows us to notice and focus on what we want to hear and filter out what we do not want to hear.

The ear's ability to attend to what we want to hear, and protect us from what we don't want to receive, is a very important ability because it would be unbearable to live surrounded by constant noise. We tune out our internal body noises which otherwise would be quite overpowering, as well as everyday interference such as the hum of air conditioning, refrigerators, computers, and traffic.

When my children were babies, they could make the tiniest noise at night and wake me from a sound sleep. My husband rarely heard the baby noises, but would wake up instantly if he heard an unusual noise around the house. That is the miracle of the middle ear. Our ears allow us to tune-in to what is most important for us to hear and tune-out the rest so that we can sleep or focus.

The middle ear has a direct connection to the emotional center in the brain. As a result, emotional responses can affect the performance of the middle ear muscles. Hearing is passive. It's what the ear automatically does. But listening is active and in-tentional. If an individual is overwhelmed or emotionally unable or unwilling to listen, the muscles of the middle ear will respond in kind and shut out the unwanted noise or communication. If the individual is highly interested or motivated to listen, these little muscles will work overtime to make sure the message comes through loud and clear!

Children who have experienced psychological or physical trauma or illness, including a difficult birth and ear infections, may have middle ear muscles that are not working as effectively as they could be. Environmental noise can overload and shutdown the system.

As with any muscle in the body, the middle ear muscles can atrophy or become less flexible with lack of use.

The inner ear has two interconnected systems to receive and interpret sound. The first is the vestibular system, which controls our response to gravity and affects balance, movement, coordina-tion and posture. Together with our hearing, the vestibular system helps us to develop our sense of space, time, and self as a reference point. These are critical elements in internal and external organi-zation, understanding and navigating our environment, planning, and communication.

The other system of the inner ear looks like a tiny snail and is called the cochlea. It is lined with little hair cells called cilia.

Each hair cell moves in response to a particular sound frequency or pitch. The cilia are lined up like members of a choir from highest to lowest frequencies, and as with many choirs, there are more sopranos than bases. There are many more cilia that respond to high frequencies than low because these are the frequencies that are most energizing and alerting to the brain.

The cochlea has connections to many parts of the brain. It helps us discriminate or analyze:

- Lower frequencies, which stimulate lower brain functions such as balance and movement,
- Mid-range frequencies, which are characteristic of speech and related to emotions, language, and sense of well-being, and
- Higher frequencies in sound, which are energizing and provide important information for musical abilities, fine discrimination, higher thinking and learning, and capturing and maintaining our interest.

Difficulty in discriminating sounds can result in an auditory processing delay. This may cause an individual to process language more slowly, miss information, or "mishear" or misinterpret what he hears. Discriminating the fine differences in sounds is an important factor in being able to learn and use phonics for reading and spelling.

Reading also requires a refined point of reference and synchrony between the vestibular and cochlear systems. The vestibular system leads the eyes and the cochlear system discriminates sounds. A loss of synchrony will occur if the cochlea takes too long to translate the sounds.

When the ears and eyes are "out of sync," the right sound may not be put together with the right letter, resulting in reading problems and loss of meaning.

According to Alfred Tomatis, M.D., the original researcher in the field of auditory stimulation and sound therapy, the ear as a whole, with its vestibular and cochlear systems, provides about

90% of the energy that the brain needs to function optimally.[2] It is not surprising then, that when listening skills are improved, energy, motivation, and productiveness can also improve.

Action items. . .
- Go to www.LearningDisability.com.
  Under "Free Articles," read:
    * "Good Learners Are Good Listeners."
- Go to www.FixLearningSkills.com.
    * Listen to "Auditory Processing – Part 1."

Executive Function

Find out how the brain's mental manager influences attention, behavior, organization, and emotional control.

In this chapter. . .

- Why parents often do more on school projects than their child
- The vital importance that executive function plays in key areas of learning and success in school
- How correcting inefficient executive function skills can release the true potential in a child's academic and social performance

The key to self-management

"Great job, Josh! Your science project looks fantastic!" Mom congratulates Josh on a job well done, as she should. He's put a lot of work into it. But secretly, she's wondering if the parents of Josh's 5th grade classmates had to do as much organizing, planning, and strategizing on their children's projects as she did. She feels a little guilty, like she cheated, but there was no way Josh was going to be able to complete this project himself.

Josh's mom isn't the only parent who put a lot of brainpower into the science fair project, and she shouldn't feel too badly about it, as long as she was guiding Josh in doing the work and not just doing it herself. Planning and executing a long-term research project requires some pretty sophisticated executive function skills.

Since executive function doesn't fully develop until about age twenty-five, most upper elementary students need a significant amount of adult guidance on a project like this. The student's own executive function skills aren't developed enough yet to do it on his own.

Homework is an absolute battle at Braden's house. Braden's middle school has given all of the 7th graders planners to write their homework in, but Braden's is rarely filled out completely, if at all. His mom checks the homework hotline, establishes what Braden has to do, and then pushes and prods while he wastes time looking for materials and trying to figure out where to start.

When Braden finally gets down to work, he rushes through it so that he can play his video games. He's pretty irritated with his mom for making him go back and correct the careless errors he made. He hasn't yet figured out that slowing down a bit and checking himself as he goes might keep him from having to redo work.

Completed papers get stuffed in the backpack, possibly to be turned in or perhaps never to be seen again. Braden's mom simply cannot understand how Braden can do the work and then "lose" it before getting credit.

Executive function sets the stage for mature, independent action.

Good student skills such as organization, time and materials management, sequencing with time for planning, and formulation of plans and strategies for behavior are functions of the frontal lobe of the brain. They are part of what's called "executive function."

These are skills that are needed in school, often before they are fully developed in the student, and skills that many students don't develop automatically. These are life skills that can be taught but rarely are. They are just assumed.

Executive function is like the Chief Executive Officer of a company. It is the person's own personal CEO. It guides and directs his behavior, helps him organize, plan, and make decisions. It reasons, strategizes, and evaluates. Everyone makes mistakes – lots of them – but thank goodness we have executive function, because this part of our thinking allows us to evaluate what went wrong and make adjustments and different decisions in the future. It allows us to be flexible and adjust to change, to change our mind and take a different course of action, or to think about things in different ways.

Executive function helps in the classroom and social situations.

Executive function is our attention monitor. Sammy is sitting in class. He really wants to ask Jennifer sitting next to him what she's doing after school today, but his executive function helps him inhibit his impulse to tap her on the shoulder and return his attention back to the teacher.

Jackie has had her hand up for several minutes waiting to be called on. She really wants to just blurt out, "Call on me already! I know the answer." But she doesn't. Her executive function warns her that that would be inappropriate and rude, so she sighs and waits her turn.

Timothy is bored. He really doesn't want to study for his Spanish test. He turns on the TV and starts flipping the channels. He looks back at his book and then picks up his phone to text message his friend. It's getting pretty late, and Timothy isn't prepared for the test that he has first thing in the morning. His executive function skills aren't strong, so he can't seem to keep himself from getting distracted and off task.

Executive function is like the little angel sitting on our shoulder whispering in our ear to guide and manage our behavior. Christy had a difficult anatomy class. The teacher had a strong accent and was very hard to understand. Christy hated the class and really wanted to give up, but her little EF Angel reminded her that failing the class would not be a good move and helped her consider other options.

She decided that reading the chapter before going to class, even though it wasn't assigned might help her understand the teacher better. She gave it a try and found that it was a helpful strategy, so she continued to use it throughout the semester.

Sue was humiliated because her boyfriend broke up with her in front of everyone at lunch. She wanted to throw her lunch at him, but the little voice in her head warned her that that this would make her feel even more stupid and conspicuous. She decided on a different course of action and walked out of the cafeteria. As she mentally reviews what happened, she doesn't feel better about the break up, but at least she didn't embarrass herself more.

Frank has a research paper due next Tuesday. It's a whole week away, so he figures he doesn't need to think about it yet. In fact, he doesn't think ahead or plan very well, so he doesn't actually remember that he has the paper until Monday night, at about 9:00 p.m. Now his parents are furious with him for putting things off until the last minute.

Frank doesn't actually say to himself, "Gee, I think I'll wait until the last minute on this project so I can infuriate my parents again," he just doesn't have a good ability to think ahead, plan a course of action, and follow it through; executive function skills that would greatly help his predicament.

Learning to manage oneself is a skill that develops over time.

Many of the learning skills that we have talked about previously, such as attention, memory, visual and motor skills development, and phonemic awareness develop very early and are fairly well in place by about eight-and-a-half years old. Executive function begins to become apparent around 4th grade but continues developing well into adulthood.

Parents and teachers do a lot to manage children's time, organization, long-term projects, and choices in elementary school because these young developing brains do not yet have the executive function to manage those things adequately.

When students get into middle school or junior high, they are better prepared to learn executive function skills, but most of them will not have good skills at this age without guidance. Middle school is considered a notoriously difficult age. Perhaps the reason for this is that these children have maturing bodies and a desire for independence that their executive function skills have not yet caught up with. Parents and teachers mistakenly think they are ready to *act* as mature as they look.

Executive function is more evident in high school students, particularly as they near their junior or senior year, but again, many students do not develop good skills in this area without specific instruction, particularly with regard to study skills and time and materials management.

Listening to the inner voice

Students with learning or attention challenges are particularly susceptible to difficulties with executive function, as executive function is quite complex and relies on solid underlying neuro-developmental skills. Inner language, which is a strong component of working memory, is an integral part of executive function.

We guide our behavior with our verbal inner language. Peter knows his mom wants him to have his homework done before she gets home from work at 5:30 p.m. He looks at the clock and sees that it's 4:00 p.m. The voice in his head says, "I'd better turn off the TV and get going on my homework or I won't have it done before Mom gets home, and then I'll be in trouble." People without this active inner voice miss out on important self-guidance.

Our visual inner language allows us to visualize how something should look or be organized and to see other points of view or possibilities. Jackson is supposed to come up with a way to illustrate the conflicting views of the three main characters in a story. He visualizes a chart he could make on his computer to show the three viewpoints but thinks it looks too boring. He imagines a cartoon graphic and decides to try that approach.

Poor visualization skills may cause students to feel stuck because they cannot imagine or try out possibilities in their mind.

Organization of time, materials, and multiple steps or tasks, are critical executive function skills for school, work, and life. There are many pre-requisite skills, such as using our inner voice and visualization, that we often assume are in place that are needed for successful planning and organization.

Lack of executive function can undermine a child's best efforts.

Carson was a high school junior who was getting average grades in advanced placement classes by having a strong enough intellect to do well on tests. He did poorly on homework because he so often forgot to do or turn in parts of the assignments. It took him a long time to get started on things, and very often, he didn't follow through to the finish.

You would assume that a smart sixteen-year-old could plan and use an assignment calendar, so his refusal to use one looked like stubbornness or laziness. He insisted that he could remember what he had to do and didn't need to write it down. To our surprise, the first time we showed him an assignment calendar that we wanted him to use to get his homework written down, he had no idea what it was. He literally couldn't "see" how it was organized and was completely overwhelmed by it.

Carson had a very poor sense of space. Even in his environment, he didn't see how things were organized. He would run into furniture walking across the room because he did not perceive that it was in his way. He would have to take everything out of his drawers every single time he wanted to find something.

Carson also had a very poor sense of time. He didn't know how much time it would take to do common everyday things. He couldn't calculate about how long it should take him to get ready for school in the morning. He didn't have a sense of how much time he needed to get to and from school, or how long any of his assignments would take to complete. He had no idea why the assignment calendar was divided into days and times; he simply could not conceptualize it.

Carson learned to use a planner, but before he could do that, he had to learn to think with time. How long was a minute, five minutes, or an hour? What did his day look like? How was it sequenced, and how long did each activity take?

When it comes to organization, students are typically given a tool, such as a calendar or a planner, and told to use it. If they don't, rather than assuming disinterest or laziness, we need to explore what pre-requisite skills might be blocking their ability to follow through as expected.

Lack of executive function can reveal itself in many ways.

Children with weak executive function skills can be difficult for parents and teachers to understand. They may have a solid set of academic skills, yet consistently be underachieving in school.

Pat was a bright, charming, confident thirteen-year-old who never picked up a book unless he absolutely had to, did the minimum he could get away with on writing assignments, and often only partially answered questions on tests and school work. For example, if the question said, "Compare the political climate in France to that of England at the beginning of the French Revolution," Pat might write about the political climate in France during the French Revolution, completely missing the word *compare* and never mentioning England.

His parents and teachers were concerned about his less than stellar performance, and Pat, who had extremely high expectations for himself, was secretly anxious about his underachievement and covered what he viewed as inadequacy by acting bored and annoyed that his parents were always on his back.

When we began working with Pat, we saw classic symptoms of executive function challenges. He read extremely fast. He read with enough intonation to trick the listener into thinking he was reading well, when in fact he was overlooking punctuation, sometimes whole phrases, and changing a number of words and endings that subtly impacted meaning.

Pat was a very verbal and articulate young man, so he could give an account of what he read that sounded great on the surface. But on careful reflection, it was evident that his speedy reading had given him a few key details to hang onto but not a good understanding of the main idea and the author's more abstract intent.

He could give quite an impressive discourse on any question, molding the same spotty details to sound like he knew what he was talking about. As Pat began to be able to regulate his reading speed, monitor his reading accuracy, and focus on the big picture of the story along with the key details, he began to pick up books for enjoyment.

One of his dad's goals had been for Pat to read a piece of "legitimate" literature, finish the book, and actually be able to have an intelligent discussion about it. While this wasn't high on Pat's priority list, he did end up doing this, and his inquisitive mind found the book quite interesting.

Pat did not come across as having a rigid personality, but we found when working with him that he was quite inflexible in his thinking. He knew he was smart and expected himself to appear that way, so he became easily frustrated with challenging tasks and resisted anything that pushed him outside his comfort zone.

He was very inflexible about trying another way or a different strategy and staunchly supported his initial idea or way of approaching a problem or a task. He was a negotiator and quite clever about it, in fact, so he'd learned to charm or wheedle his way out of just about anything.

Pat often came into sessions extremely tired. Granted, he was playing club sports at night and his sessions were early, so he had a reason to be tired. But what we noticed was that reading and writing tasks caused him to be particularly sleepy, in spite of having been highly alert and energized as he walked in the room from his break.

He started bringing caffeine-loaded high-energy drinks into sessions to help him stay awake, which of course, we wouldn't let him have. Pat was a good sport about it and found as his own awareness, self-monitoring, and control increased, he didn't need the drinks to keep himself alert.

Even though he was a voracious talker, Pat had difficulty expressing himself clearly and concisely, both orally and in writing. He tended to confuse quantity with quality, feeling that the more words he said or wrote the better. What typically happened was that that the main point got lost or became vague. His challenges with attention and working memory contributed to this problem because he tended to feel like he had to speak or write quickly or he would forget what he wanted to say.

As we worked with Pat, he greatly increased in his understanding and awareness of taking time before responding so that he could think carefully about his wording and say exactly what he wanted the listener or reader to know. He also became more aware of himself and of thinking before he acted. This helped him curb his impulsiveness and make better decisions.

Pat had a large summer literature project. Segments of it had to be turned-in in increments, and the final project was due to his 8th grade English teacher before the start of school. He had been using typical but inefficient strategies to attack that project, strategies like reading the material over and over again, hoping it would sink in; the panic strategy of waiting to the last minute to work on the next segment due so that the adrenaline pushed him to get it done;

working on a long-term project without any kind of a time table or plan other than the increment due dates; and negative self-talk.

While his mind was focusing on things like, "It's so unfair that we have to do all this work over the summer," and "I wish my mom would quit bugging me about this project," processing of anything else was impossible. Not a very productive strategy for getting the project done.

As Pat's executive function skills improved, he began to recognize that his negotiating and complaining was a strategy to get him out of things that he didn't want to do. He became more flexible and willing to try new things, and along with this came better independent follow through.

When Pat finished his six-week intensive program at the learning center, he was more able to deal with frustration and approached challenging tasks with much less resistance. He hadn't completely let go of the negotiating strategy that had protected him so well over the years, but he was aware of it and didn't rely on it nearly as much. Awareness is an important first step in making a different decision.

10 signs of deficient executive function

Pat presents quite a remarkable case study because he was experiencing inefficiency in so many of the key areas of executive function. These are listed below.

1. Inefficiency with understanding and applying learning and test vocabulary

There is a whole set of vocabulary that supports a student in learning and testing. If students don't understand and utilize these words and concepts, they will have inefficiency in their strategies for learning the material and understanding test questions. *Learning Vocabulary* includes words and concepts such as: visualize, inner voice, thinking, main idea, concentrate, study, and goal. *Testing vocabulary* includes these words: explain, compare, contrast, define, diagram, discuss, and illustrate.

2. Poor self-monitoring of the quality of performance or work

Lack of internal quality control will lead to errors in understanding, underachievement, and lack of independence in education.

Learning to pay attention to exactly what they are saying and doing, as well as developing strategies for double checking and self-correcting their work, helps students be much more successful in both the classroom and social arena.

3. Poor regulation of working speed

The ability to assess the appropriate working rate for a task is an important executive function skill that allows students to budget their time and allot the appropriate amount of energy and focus to various tasks. Pat's perception was that *fast* meant intelligent. When he was able to monitor and regulate his speed, he was able to show his intelligence with more balanced, productive, and accurate performance.

4. Mental inflexibility and poor problem-solving strategies

Every arena of life involves problem solving. Poor executive function skills will cause a person to have difficulty thinking logically and having the mental flexibility to see other points of view and examine options. This not only creates roadblocks to higher learning academically, but also causes problems socially, as these children, teens, or adults rigidly demand to do things their own way.

5. Poor emotional regulation and control

Emotional resilience is an important aspect of executive function. It allows students to rebound quickly after a disappointing performance and persevere in their efforts without going overboard or getting overwhelmed.

Pat was actually quite anxious and self-conscious about his under-performance academically and diverted attention from it by affecting an attitude of complacency or being the life of the party. As his executive function improved, he became more balanced and rational in his responses. He could recognize his coping strategies for what they were and make different choices.

6. Poor use of inner language and working memory strategies

This can cause students who understand the material as they are reading or hearing it to have difficulty remembering it, taking notes, or answering questions at the end of the chapter.

7. Poor ability to self-regulate alertness

Students with this challenge use a great deal of energy fighting to keep themselves alert. As a result, attention and focus are siphoned off from listening, reading, and learning efficiency. We worked with a college student who had quit college twice by the time we met him for exactly this reason. While he was working on his program at the learning center, he re-registered for classes and successfully completed his semester.

8. Inability to use strategies or use of ineffective strategies

Understanding what strategies are, how to develop them, and how to use them helps students to use their time, attention, and energy resources more efficiently.

9. Poor planning and organization skills

Managing homework, studying for tests, and organizing and completing long-term projects require a number of specific skills, including the ability to choose a project, think and sequence with time, manage materials, generate ideas independently, and plan and take the appropriate steps necessary to perform most effectively.

10. Unclear or ineffective language expression

Inability to express ideas clearly, to the point, and in logical order can get in the way of social communication, written language, and successful participation in discussions, group projects, and oral presentations. Clear and direct language expression is also an important factor in the inner language that guides and manages our behavior and attention.

Executive function can be learned.

Children with executive function challenges are often underachieving academically and suffering socially. The problems are not as obvious and definitive as not being able to read, so they may be mistaken for attitude or lack of motivation, when in fact, these students are doing the best they can. They are told to behave, to study, or to pay attention, but they are rarely taught how.

The *how* is the critical factor. Executive function abilities are high-level neurodevelopmental learning skills. They can be taught and improved. Students with executive function challenges not only need to be given strategies and structure, but they need to be taught *how* to recognize and self-monitor their attention, *how* to create and evaluate strategies to match their needs, *how* to use their inner language effectively, and *how* to reason and solve problems.

Pat's inefficiencies with executive function caused him to have to put out excessive effort to meet expectations at school, yet still left him working below his intellectual potential. Developing new understandings and habits allowed him to be more independent and successful when he started 8th grade in the fall.

Action items. . .
- Go to www.LearningDisability.com.
  Under "Free Articles," read:
    * "Pacing – Somewhere Between Racing and Crawling."
    * "How to Win the Homework Battle."

CHAPTER 12

Succeeding in School

What are the basic academic skills that students need in order to be successful in school, and why are they such a struggle for some children? What does it take to be good in reading, writing, spelling, and math?

In this chapter. . .
- The skills that contribute to success in reading, writing, spelling, and math
- The signals that a skill is underdeveloped
- How a deficiency in one skill affects other skills
- What students achieve when they are working on a solid foundation of academic skills

Academic challenges begin with poor learning skills.
We have established that the primary reason students struggle in school is weak or underdeveloped supporting learning skills. Fixing or strengthening these learning skills is the first step in correcting academic problems. Once learning skills are corrected, the academics may fall into place all on their own, but for many students, some degree of academic remediation will be needed.

Let's take a look at the foundational academic skills that allow students to be successful in school, and what sub-skills are needed to be good at them.

Reading

The number one reason parents call our learning center for help is because their child is struggling with reading. Reading has three main components: phonics, sight words, and comprehension. Because English is a phonetic language, understanding and being able to automatically use the phonetic code is critical to successful reading.

The auditory processing skill that provides the brain with the information needed to learn and use phonics is called phonemic awareness, or the ability to think about the sounds in words. Research tells us that phonemic awareness is the key predictor of success or failure in reading.

Sight words are words that have been recorded in long-term memory. The reader recognizes them instantly by sight. If a learner has difficulty with phonics, his sight vocabulary will often be weak as well. Words become sight words by being decoded or read accurately enough times that they are automatically recognized.

The reason we read is to comprehend. If a student is very inaccurate in her reading, or if too much energy is being put into reading the words, her comprehension may be compromised.

If any of the three key components of reading – phonics, sight words, or comprehension – is weak, the person will not be as efficient a reader as he could be. Over the years, I have often heard teachers say, "I have students who can't learn phonics. They just don't seem to hear the sounds, so we teach them by sight."

It has been a popular notion to focus on a person's strengths to try to get around his weak areas. But if we choose to eliminate any aspect of reading, we are opting for that student to be a less efficient reader than he could be and to always have to work harder at it than he should.

Daniel was a college student on a break when he came in for testing. He was very bright and maintained grades that placed him on the Dean's Honor Roll. But he knew that there was something wrong. He had to work so much harder and longer than his peers.

Testing showed that Daniel had excellent comprehension and a very strong visual memory that had allowed him to memorize a lot of words. His phonetic decoding, however, was at a second grade level, and he had extremely weak phonemic awareness. No wonder he had to work so hard. He was using his comprehension and sight vocabulary to compensate, but he was missing the other third of the reading process.

Daniel was so excited that there was actually something wrong—a real reason why he was having to work so hard—not that he just wasn't that smart. He only had three weeks before he left again for school. In that time, Daniel worked intensively to improve his phonemic awareness and phonics skills and returned to school as a much more efficient reader.

Many times when students can read but are struggling with accuracy and fluency, they do poorly with reading tests and reading comprehension questions. Parents call us saying that their child has trouble with reading comprehension. In our evaluation, we always want to determine if what they are seeing is truly a comprehension problem or a reading problem.

Reading comprehension

Allie is a college-bound senior. She is outstanding in math and sciences. She is low average in reading. She hates to read and does poorly on reading comprehension tests. However, her listening comprehension is excellent. She has a good vocabulary and can reason with language.

Allie does not have a reading comprehension problem. She has a reading problem. Her reading comprehension scores are low because her decoding skills are so weak and her sight vocabulary is so mediocre that she makes numerous word reading errors in every paragraph. This affects her comprehension. Once her word reading challenges are cleared up, she shouldn't have any further trouble with comprehension and will probably even begin to enjoy reading.

Edwin, on the other hand, has a true reading comprehension deficit. He can read the words, but he reads in a monotone voice, with no attention to meaning or punctuation. He has great difficulty understanding vocabulary and thinking beyond the very concrete meaning in the passages. He has these same challenges when listening. Edwin's difficulties have to be addressed in a completely different way than Allie's.

Edwin's program is focusing on auditory stimulation and specific comprehension and reasoning strategies that are helping him not only with reading comprehension, but with understanding lectures, and conversations as well. As his overall comprehension has improved, he has become more social, more connected in class, and more independent with homework.

Spelling

Students with reading problems often have spelling difficulties as well. Being a good speller depends upon understanding the phonetic code of the language and requires knowing what words look like. There are many letters or letter combinations in English that can be used to spell more than one sound, and there are many sounds with more than one spelling.

Good spellers are able to determine what sounds are in the word and mentally image, or picture, the correct spelling. As students are checking their spelling when writing, we encourage them to use these questions: 1) Does it *sound* right? and 2) Does it *look* right? People who read a lot will tend to be better spellers simply because they are exposed to more words more often. Repeated exposure to correctly spelled words helps anchor the image in long-term memory.

When reading and spelling are both being remediated, we often see that reading progresses faster than spelling. Comprehension and the flow of the language support the reader's decoding and sight word recognition. There is no comprehension component to help access the spelling.

We sometimes find with spelling that as students learn to think about the sounds and use phonics rules, their spelling goes from being primarily memorized to being phonetic. They may begin to make mistakes with words they know because they are trying to spell them phonetically.

This alarms parents, but it is really just a step in the process. The student has learned some new skills and is not yet adept at applying them along with what he already knows. As students are taught how to think about both the visual and phonetic aspects of spelling, they integrate their new learning with existing skills and the errors diminish and end.

Speech, language, and reading

Many times, children who had early speech and language delays end up having reading problems. Speech, language, and reading share many of the same underlying auditory processing skills. It makes sense that if a child can't "hear" the sounds in words in order to say them, he will also struggle to read them. Early warning signs of possible phonemic awareness and reading problems are difficulties with rhyming, mispronunciation of words, and lack of word play in young children.

By evaluating and properly addressing auditory processing issues early, reading problems can often be avoided completely. By the same token, properly evaluating and addressing the underlying issues causing reading problems can have the side benefit of cleaning up lingering speech, articulation, and language problems.

Language comprehension

When a child has trouble understanding what he reads *and* hears, and auditory processing and reading problems have been ruled out, he is struggling with language comprehension. Good comprehension of language requires that the person turn the words and sentences he is hearing into mental images. In a story, it would be like making a movie in his mind.

We cannot begin to remember all of the words we hear or read. There are far too many. Students who try to do this may be able to repeat back some of what they hear or read, but will typically not show good comprehension of the material.

The old adage, "A picture is worth a thousand words," is true. A great deal of information can be stored in a single picture that would take a huge number of words to explain. By imaging as we are reading or listening, we will be much more successful in understanding, storing, and retrieving the information.

The next step in language comprehension is to be able to see the gestalt, or big picture. As students are creating their mental movie of the material, they need to see how all of the frames, or individual images, fit together to make a whole. Students who over-focus on details will not be able to think about the main idea or think critically with the material. Higher-level thinking requires an understanding of the whole from which to compare, contrast, analyze, and evaluate.

Understanding of vocabulary within context and careful attention to punctuation, intonation, wording, and the author or speaker's intent all contribute to comprehension. Logic and reasoning skills are higher-level comprehension skills and form an overlap with executive function.

Students who have difficulty with language comprehension often run into social problems. We worked with a teacher as a client who had serious listening and language comprehension problems. She was a very nice woman, but because she did not comprehend well, she talked a lot and talked around things in a very vague manner. Listening to her and trying to decipher the message she was trying to get across was hard work and caused people to not want to talk to her. She felt like her colleagues didn't like her, but she didn't understand why.

Mike's comprehension problems affected him very differently. His biggest issue was seeing the gestalt, or the big picture. When he would go out on the playground, he couldn't easily see the big picture of what was happening, who was grouped up in a private conversation, and which games were more open for others to join. As a result, he often barged in where he wasn't wanted. Mike had difficulty following and participating in conversations because he couldn't follow the thread of the conversation that tied the different comments together. To him, it all felt random.

Mike participated in an auditory stimulation and training program that used a combination of specific music selections and visualizing and reasoning techniques that helped him to organize information so he could understand the "whole" and the relationships between people, events, and ideas. This had a profound effect on him. Understanding his world more accurately transformed Mike from an extremely quiet, anxious, dependent child to an outgoing, confident, and independent student.

Written language

Written language can be quite challenging for students who have any kind of learning skills delay because there are so many components to deal with. To be good at written language, the student has to be able to:

- Come up with an idea
- Visualize the gestalt or whole idea of what she wants to say
- Organize her thoughts in sub-topics with supporting details
- Prioritize her ideas
- Generate the words and appropriate vocabulary
- Express her ideas clearly and succinctly
- Sequence words and ideas in a logical order
- Extend her ideas and use interesting language
- Use handwriting or keyboarding automatically and accurately
- Spell automatically and at the level of her oral language
- Use grammar correctly
- Edit for flow, content, and clarity, and
- Proofread for capitalization, punctuation, and spelling.

There are many pre-requisite skills to each of these sub-skills of written language. Schools and tutors can do a good job of teaching written language skills, but when a student struggles in spite of good instruction, it is time to take a deeper look.

A targeted evaluation can help pinpoint where in the writing process skills are breaking down and what underlying processing skills are not supporting the learner well enough. Correcting the underlying weaknesses in attention, memory, visual, auditory, motor, language, and/or comprehension skills first, makes learning and applying written language skills infinitely easier.

Handwriting

Handwriting is a lost art in most schools in the United States. This is distressing because repetitive handwriting movements create neural connections in the brain that influence impulse control, attention, reading, and learning. Jeanette Farmer, a handwriting remediation specialist, states in her book, *Train the Brain to Pay Attention the Write Way*, "That 'penmanship' or handwriting training has an inherent capacity to 'hard wire' the brain, influencing literacy in the process is a biological fact."[1]

If a child's handwriting is not automatic and subconscious by age eleven, it will interfere with learning. If conscious focus has to go into forming letters or writing legibly, attention will be drawn away from learning. Keeping up with assignments, performing quickly enough on a test, paying attention in lectures where notes are required, or any writing assignments will be affected by poor handwriting skills.

In his book, *A Mind at a Time*, Mel Levine, M.D. states, "...there are countless students with good ideas whose fingers can't keep pace with their thinking, as a result of which, they come to despise and avoid writing." [2]

Because handwriting is neurologically and practically tied in with attention and learning, we find that working on handwriting is time well-spent. It can be very difficult to break old, inefficient writing patterns because they are so ingrained. We have found that teaching handwriting skills in non-habitual ways, such as using handwriting movements instead of letters at first, moving in a progression from large to small muscle movements, and pairing the writing activity with music and rhythm helps students to develop more efficient habits and experience greater success at school.

Math

People's reaction to math varies but often is quite emphatic and negative. What is it about math that makes even well-educated adults want to run and hide when their kids ask for help? What could be so intimidating about numbers?

We have found that many students try to learn math calculations and processes without really understanding what they are all about. As a result, they have inconsistent performance and are unable to catch and correct their errors. They never really understand how math works, so it becomes something to avoid.

Math is logical and provable. Everything about it makes sense if you understand how numbers work. Learning math by rote, without a foundation of understanding does not work, at least not for very long. We find that students with comprehension problems often struggle with math. They don't understand math vocabulary and cannot easily conceptualize the organization on the page or the logic of the processes.

In our clinic, we use a multisensory step-by-step program called Discover Math™, written and researched by Dr. Stephen Truch[3], which helps students to truly understand how math and numbers work. From basic number line skills through algebra, students first use real objects, drawing, and dialoguing to explore, understand, and prove math concepts. When the same processes are then taught with numbers on paper, they make sense.

Having students explore and prove their answers and verbally describe what they are doing clearly and sequentially, improves not only math skills, but memory, mental flexibility, reasoning, comprehension, and expressive language as well.

Instruction in academic skills should typically follow development of needed underlying learning or processing skills. However, depending upon the level and degree of challenges, the learning skills development and academic remediation may be able to be done simultaneously. Testing and evaluation help determine the approach that will most quickly and effectively help the child to become a comfortable and independent learner.

Action items. . .
- Go to www.LearningDisability.com.
  Under "Free Articles," read:
  * "Breaking the He-Can't-Learn-Phonics-Myth."
  * "Tackling Spelling."
  * "So What Is Dyslexia Anyway?"
- Go to www.FixLearningSkills.com.
  * Listen to "Why Do So Many Smart Kids Have Trouble Reading?"

CHAPTER 13

Diet and Environmental Factors

Biochemical factors need to be considered

In this chapter. . .
- The impact of environmental toxins on brain chemistry and function
- The influence of diet on behavior and mental capacity
- Telltale signs of food allergies

The hidden influence on children's brains and behavior

A conversation about what triggers particular behaviors in children would not be complete without mentioning nutrition and everyday chemicals. At our center, we are alert for potential problems in this area, although we refer our clients to professionals who specialize in diet and toxins. As a parent, you will want to note that this is an often-overlooked factor when searching for root causes of learning, behavior, or attention challenges.

Biochemistry can have a dramatic effect on a child's attention, behavior, and learning and it cannot be trained. It needs to be understood and adjusted. Our bodies have a difficult time assimilating what is unnatural. Environmental toxins such as pesticides and man-made chemical additives to food have been shown to affect cognitive processing.

Heavy metal toxicity has also been shown to affect brain chemistry, and may be linked to violent behavior, autism, learning disabilities, and attention deficits. The major heavy metal toxins are lead, arsenic, mercury, cadmium, zinc, and nickel. Arsenic and mercury have been found in some seafood and some water pipes and fountains. Industrial factories continue to expose people to lead.

Blood, urine, or hair analysis tests can help detect the levels of chemicals in the body. This is the first step in eliminating the offending toxins and reducing future exposure.

Studies have shown that what we eat affects how we feel, how we think, and how much energy we have. Memory, thinking, and attention are strongly influenced by food. According to neurologist David Perlmutter, author of *The Better Brain Book*, "the standard American diet is a nightmare."[1] He goes on to say, "If I were to design a diet for the sole purpose of creating an epidemic of poor brain function, accelerated brain aging, mood disorders, and other neurological problems, it would be the one that most Americans are already following."[2]

What the brain needs most

Believe it or not, the most important nutrient for the brain is fat because the brain is actually made up of fat. The problem is, if we eat a lot of unhealthy fats, we end up with an unhealthy brain.

Fats that support brain health are monounsaturated fats (found in foods like olive oil, canola oil, nuts, and avocados), and some forms of polyunsaturated fats, including the Omega 3 essential fatty acids, which are particularly important for brain function. Omega 3 fatty acids can be found in cold water fatty fish, deep green leafy vegetables, some grains, and pumpkin seeds. Many people find it helpful to supplement their intake of these essential Omega 3s by taking fish oil capsules.

The fats to stay away from are saturated fats and trans-fatty acids. Saturated fats are found in meat and full-fat dairy products. We need protein in our diet, much of which comes from these sources, but limiting the amount of saturated fat to about 10 percent of our daily caloric intake is wise, as saturated fat makes the brain cells sluggish. According to Dr. Perlmutter, a diet high in saturated fats can result in memory problems and mood disorders for individuals of any age. It is not just seniors who are having "senior moments" these days.

Trans-fatty acids are probably the worst fats for our brains and should be on our diet black list. These are found in nearly all processed foods (partially-hydrogenated vegetable oil or partially-hydrogenated vegetable shortening) and fried foods. Trans-fatty acids are used to increase the shelf life of food but inhibit our learning and performance because they make our brain cells rigid, tough, and slow. They keep cells from being able to get nutrients, make energy, and communicate with other cells.

Carbohydrates are important foods for providing energy for the body. But just as with fats, there are good and bad choices. Sugar and white flour are two of the worst. They are simple carbohydrates, so they enter the bloodstream very quickly. They rapidly raise blood sugar levels, which is associated with memory problems. Sugar robs our bodies of B vitamins and nutrients needed to support a stable nervous system and blood sugar balance, affecting health, moods, attention, memory, and behavior.

Be aware that there is an extremely high sugar content in juice (eating the whole fruit is better) and that our bodies react to artificial sweeteners other than Stevia in the same way as sugar.

Blood sugar levels affect the brain.

Maintaining consistent blood sugar levels allows the brain to get the steady flow of sugar (glucose) needed to keep it fit and functioning. Spikes and fluctuations in blood sugar lead to sugar overload, which can cause an individual to have very high, sometimes excessive energy, followed by low energy, sleepiness, or moodiness. Over time, chronic sugar overload can lead to serious illnesses. William Duffy, author of *Sugar Blues*, says, "Excessive sugar has a strong mal-effect on the functioning of the brain. Too much sugar makes one sleepy; our ability to calculate and remember is lost."[3] This is definitely not a good prescription for learning!

Since we do need carbohydrates for energy and to help protein (in the form of tryptophan) enter the brain cells, complex carbohydrates will be the better choice. These digest more slowly, enter the bloodstream more gradually, and create a gentler rise in blood sugar. Whole grains, fruits, legumes, and vegetables are complex carbohydrates.

Protein is extremely important to our brain function and learning. It helps increase serotonin in the brain which improves feelings of well-being, hopefulness, organization, and concentration.

Many children go to school after having a sugary carbohydrate breakfast, and many teens choose to go to school with no breakfast at all. A low sugar breakfast and lunch with 12–20 grams of protein can make a vast difference in a learner's performance.

Is your child allergic to dairy?

Doris Rapp, M.D., presents numerous case studies in her book *Is This Your Child?* that suggest that allergies can be a key factor in medical, personality, and learning problems and that dairy is one of the foods that most frequently causes allergies.[4]

Dr. Joan Smith, author and researcher, looked for many years at the connections between allergies or sensitivities to dairy and sugar and learning and attention challenges. In one case study, she documents a change in receptive language scores from the 2nd percentile to the 63rd percentile following an intervention of removing dairy and sugar from the diet. Changes in attention, response time, and IQ scores as a result of eliminating dairy and sugar, have been documented in Dr. Smith's book, *Learning Victories*.[5] In our practice, we also have seen a strong correlation between dairy and sugar and response time.

Food allergies can cause headaches, fatigue, drowsiness, poor concentration, short attention span, hyperactivity, and irritability. Parents can be watching for the following signs of food allergies:

1. Dark circle under the eyes
2. Puffiness under the eyes
3. Muscle aches
4. Digestive problems
5. Dry, itchy skin; eczema; bumps on the arms, legs, or face
6. Chronic stuffy nose; sinus problems
7. Asthma

The culprit foods in food allergies and sensitivities are usually the child's "must have" foods, those that the child craves.

The elimination diet reveals allergies.

Most parents we speak to feel that their child has a pretty good diet. It might make an interesting experiment for the parents to eat *exactly* what their child eats for a week to see how they feel. Parents can also try doing an elimination diet to see what foods their child appears to react to. This involves completely eliminating *all* of the child's favorite foods. You have to check food labels very carefully in order to do this, as key allergens such as dairy, wheat, corn, peanuts, and soy are in a multitude of foods.

On the elimination diet, the child's behavior may get worse for a few days, but by day four or five, the behavior should improve. The system is then challenged by giving the child only one suspect food at a time to see if the behavior reverts.[6]

Making dietary changes can be an important component of a child's total program for improving learning skills. This is easiest to do with professional guidance from a health care professional who specializes in nutrition in relation to attention, behavior, and learning.

It's important to realize that there's not usually just one single issue that is the culprit in a learning problem, and while it would be great to have a "silver bullet" or a "magic pill," there rarely is one. Using the learning skills continuum along with exploring nutritional factors can help us understand the roots of the challenge and create a plan for correcting them.

In Part 2, we will be exploring some of the highly effective strategies and programs that can be used to close the gaps in students' underlying learning skills so they can become the learners they have the potential to be.

Action items. . .

- Go to www.LearningDisability.com.
  Under "Free Articles," read:
    * "Healthy Brain Habits."
    * "7 Easy Ways to Make the School Year More Fun and Productive."

The Learning Skills Continuum Approach to Solving Learning Problems

When we understand the learning skills continuum and see how a child's academic struggles relate back to specific levels on the continuum, we then have the roadmap for fixing the weak learning skills and getting the student on the path to successful and independent learning.

I have always said that my strength was not in inventing things, but in finding the things that other people were doing that really worked and putting them together in even more efficient and effective ways for our students.

In Part Two, you will learn about the strategies and programs we have found to be the most successful in developing the underlying skills students of all ages must have in order to be successful learners. Some of the programs have been developed in our clinic; others have not. For those programs that we have developed, I am forever indebted to my mentors in the field, who have shared their knowledge so generously and have such passion for children with learning challenges.

Shortly after starting the learning center in 1984, I was fortunate to meet and train with Pat and Phyllis Lindamood. They taught me that reading problems were often the result of an underdeveloped thinking process called phonemic awareness. If this thinking process wasn't addressed, the student and instructor would spin their wheels trying to correct the reading problem. But when the brain was able to process or get the information that it should, reading could be learned easily.

Since that time, I have had many wonderful mentors who ignited my passion and guided my learning.

Let's take a look at solutions.

CHAPTER 14

The Learning Skills Continuum Approach to Solving Learning Problems

Find out how using this approach can make dramatic changes in your child's learning, even when nothing else has worked.

In this chapter. . .

- How using the Learning Skills Continuum Approach can help identify and address the roadblocks to a person's learning
- How the approach can be adapted to a variety of challenges a child has
- The transformative effect the approach can have for both children and parents

"You can either dilute the learning or fortify the learner!" *R. Feuerstein, M.D.*

We have no interest in diluting the learning. Children and adults with average to above average intelligence can and should be comfortable and independent learners. They should not limp along through school or life, underachieving and working too hard and too long for minimal outcomes. Our goal is help students correct the problem, not just cope or compensate for their learning differences. This involves three steps:

1. Identify the underlying skills that are weak or not supporting the learning well enough.
2. Specifically and intensively attack and strengthen these areas of underlying weakness so that brain gets better information to think and learn with.
3. Remediate and close the gaps in the student's basic academic skills (reading, writing, spelling, and math).

In the remaining chapters, we will be looking at what we call the *Learning Skills Continuum Approach* to solving learning problems and several of the key programs that are used in it. In the past twenty-five years, we have seen thousands of children and adults turn their learning and future around by using this approach in determining and developing the learning skills they need to be successful.

We are talking here about individuals with average to above average intelligence whose difficulties in school would fall under the umbrella of dyslexia, specific learning disability, ADD/ADHD, and non-diagnosed learning and attention challenges. We are not specifically talking about students with low cognitive function, which is the source of their slow learning style or mental retardation. We are also not specifically addressing Autistic Spectrum Disorders. However, students in both of these populations have gotten great benefit from both the continuum-based approach and the specific programming that we will be addressing.

We use a continuum approach because it gives us the biggest overall picture of learning. If we want students to develop to their potential and be able to learn and flourish as they should in education and in life, we must understand what the building blocks are, where the breakdowns are occurring, and where to start so that no time is wasted and all bases are covered. The Learning Skills Continuum provides us a tool to do that.

Putting the puzzle pieces together

We met Amy in Chapter 7. By sixteen years old, she was very behind academically and socially. In spite of trying very hard, Amy was a puzzle to her teachers and was making very little progress in her full day special education class. Amy had been getting academic support and remediation throughout her school years, but no significant difference in her learning and performance had been made.

Amy came to the learning center to do a six-week intensive program over the summer. Using the Learning Skills Continuum Approach, it was clear that before academic remediation could be effective, Amy's core learning skills and auditory processing delays had to be addressed. Because she was doing an intensive program, overall processing skills development, which would have been her next step, was done simultaneously.

Parents help us monitor and document changes. Here are comments from Amy's mom following her first day of Samonas Sound Therapy[1], a component of the Auditory Stimulation and Training[2] program Amy was doing within her summer intensive.

"As requested, Amy began the sound therapy for twenty-four minutes on Friday. The results were immediate and amazing! She was calmer, anticipated and planned her moves, and was much more organized. Her math teacher noticed a marked difference as well. In the afternoon, Amy seemed very tired. Aside from the drowsiness, I have seen some really positive social changes already. She is smiling (a very rare event) and asked to help with dinner. [This is the first time anyone] has really understood and begun to target the problem."

After 3 weeks Amy's mom reported, "Amy's self-esteem has greatly improved since beginning [at the learning center]. She makes her own decisions and is much more self-directed. She is aware of the little details now. She stands straighter and is much less fidgety and nervous. She laughs now.

"The most obvious improvement and growth has been in the social and emotional area. Amy seems so much more age-appropriate now. She listens and doesn't interrupt as much. She volunteers information and is more verbal with a better vocabulary. Huge gains in this area!

"Amy has finished two books in two weeks! She has always avoided reading before, and now, we schedule regular library trips.

"I have always felt so alone with my daughter's struggles. Nobody else seemed to 'get it.' Thank you for helping my daughter realize that she can learn—and quickly. She has blossomed before my eyes into a confident, smiling, laughing teenager. No one has ever been able to help her with that before."

This is exactly why using the Learning Skills Continuum Approach to resolving learning challenges is so valuable. It helps us to wade through the symptoms and "get" the problem. Amy had had help before—lots of it, and for years—but it wasn't targeting the right issues. But in three weeks, she made dramatic changes. Why?

The Learning Skills Continuum helps us to understand where the roadblocks to learning are, what areas need to be improved or developed through retraining the brain, and where to begin. Amy is now working on academic skills remediation with the goal of passing the high school exit exam and going to college to be a veterinarian. She has a ways to go, but I think she'll make it. Everyday, she is becoming more and more the person she has the potential to be. That's what the Learning Skills Continuum Approach is all about.

Using the Learning Skills Continuum helps practitioners determine a starting point and treatment protocol. We'll use Tyler and Shawn to help illustrate this.

Overcoming problems from infancy

Tyler was in a regular second grade class at school. He was performing very well, considering his early health history. Tyler was born with very low birth weight and low chances of survival. He had several surgeries in the first few weeks after birth, which kept him immobile for three months.

At eight years old, Tyler was a very quiet little boy. He didn't speak much, and when he did, it was difficult for others to understand him because his speech was so unclear. Tyler was able to read, write, and do math, but he was behind most of the other children in his class in all areas.

Testing confirmed the presence of neurodevelopmental delay. Since primitive reflexes are integrated through repetitive movements that babies make, neurodevelopmental delay would be expected for Tyler due to his health problems and immobility as an infant. He also appeared to have poor listening skills centered mainly around getting an accurate and complete message the first time he heard it. Phonemic awareness was poor and seemed to play a part in this.

Tyler appeared to need a listening "warm-up period." He seemed attentive while directions were being given, but would miss the beginning part of the instructions so that he needed to have things repeated or clarified. Tyler was a very sensitive child, and at points in the testing, looked like he was going to cry.

Many of Tyler's processing skills scores were good, but his responses were very inconsistent. He correctly answered and missed both easy and difficult items. This is usually related to attention challenges, but did not appear to be attention in Tyler's case.

Tyler needed to begin his learning skills intervention with Core Learning Skills Training[3] and Auditory Stimulation and Training. The Core Learning Skills Training would integrate the retained primitive reflexes and help build the internal organization, motor, visual, and mental control that were not able to become stable and automatic because of the neurological interference of the reflexes. Improvements in these areas would help reduce Tyler's sensitivity and increase his confidence and consistency.

Auditory Stimulation and Training was used along with Core Learning Skills Training for two reasons. The first was to support the motor and visual skills development. Stimulating the auditory system also stimulates the vestibular system, since it is housed in the inner ear. This is our center for balance, movement, and response to gravity. Sound therapy, which is a part of Auditory Stimulation and Training, is a very powerful tool in helping students develop a reference point, sense of self, and sense of balance, control, and movement.

The second purpose for starting Auditory Stimulation and Training right away was that Tyler's language and communication were being affected by his poor listening skills.

Following his core learning and auditory stimulation programs, Tyler was ready to work on higher-level auditory and visual skills, along with memory, attention, logic and reasoning, and processing speed in a processing skills program called PACE[4] *(Processing and Cognitive Enhancement)*. As the result of his continuum-based interventions, Tyler became happier and more confident, outgoing, and at ease with himself. He engaged more and was interactive in conversations. He loved to tell stories and was much less vague when he spoke. Tyler also started asking lots of questions and was able to shift gears with greater ease.

Tyler's ability to think about the sounds in words improved. He was able to decode better and read faster. Improved listening skills and decoding allowed Tyler to get more accurate and complete information to think with, which allowed him to grasp stories and concepts with greater ease and accuracy. Tyler made such transformations in his life and learning as a result of improving his core learning, auditory processing, and overall processing skills, that the academic skills came together for him on their own.

Starting with academic remediation instead of at the core learning skills level would not have had the same result, and likely would have ended up with Tyler feeling additional anxiety over reading and school. Instead, he was much less anxious toward learning and more willing to try challenging tasks without getting overwhelmed.

Dyslexia no longer a hindrance

Cute, coordinated, and confident described Shawn, a thirteen-year-old athlete and actor, who also happened to be dyslexic. He had weak auditory processing, which affected his phonetic decoding, overall reading, spelling, auditory memory, and confidence for anything written.

Shawn had confusion with similar letters and words and sequencing of letters and numbers. His visual processing was better than his auditory processing but was not strong. In spite of the initial confidence that Shawn showed, he became extremely anxious about reading. He did not show signs of retained reflexes or delayed core-learning skills.

Shawn's program began with Auditory Stimulation and Training and processing skills development. He did not need to start at the earliest level on the continuum as Tyler did, but because his challenges had a very specific impact on reading and spelling, he needed to go into reading and spelling remediation following his processing skills training. Shawn's underlying learning skills challenges had caused him to miss critical reading skills when they were taught.

Eliminating anxiety about learning

Tyler was able to learn basic academic skills including reading, but his weak underlying skills kept him from accessing and using the information he had learned with any efficiency. Shawn's weak processing skills had kept him developing good basic reading skills. Both boys show a significant amount of anxiety related to learning.

For Tyler, this was addressed through Core Learning Skills Training, which eliminated the neurological interference that kept him constantly feeling a little "off-base."

For Shawn, the anxiety diminished as he was better able to process sounds in words and be more successful with reading. He was happy that easier reading and better memorization turned out to be outcomes of his training. He felt he could memorize scripts more quickly, which was an important goal that he had for himself when he began his summer program. Shawn also said that his reaction time in sports was quicker.

Training the brain leads to success.

The Learning Skills Continuum Approach has a completely different feel than traditional teaching or tutoring. It is highly interactive and is much more about developing the *how* or process of learning than the *what* or knowledge. The Learning Skills Continuum provides a framework for neuro-cognitive training. It is about training brains, whether the starting point is high-level executive function skills or lower-level reflex integration and body skills, to improve awareness, mental flexibility, and control for optimal learning and functioning.

This requires getting good information from the eyes, ears, body, and movement, and perceiving it accurately. In this approach, the learner is highly engaged. Even at a very young age, we want to guide students in understanding what they are feeling and doing and how they are thinking.

This is training, not testing. We are not after right answers, right responses, or right movements all of the time. We are after increased conscious awareness and control. When we deal with attention, it is not about making a student pay attention so that we can teach him, but about helping him learn how to internally recognize and gain control of attention so that he can be taught.

A high-level athlete must be very aware of her body, position in space, timing, movements, and thinking. Athletes train hard to gain the level of mental and physical control and flexibility needed to be competitive. One of our daughter's ice skating coaches told her that each jump that she learned would come after about a thousand falls. This is training: trying, awareness, adjusting, trying again. The Learning Skills Continuum Approach utilizes neuro-cognitive training to build a stable foundation of learning skills at all levels.

A different way that works

A wonderful book called *Hooray for Diffendoofer Day* based on sketches by Theodore "Dr. Seuss" Geisel and written by Jack Prelutsky was released after the death of the beloved Dr. Seuss. It is the story of a wild and wacky teacher who pushes her class to explore and make noise and move and experiment and try out crazy notions.

One day, the principal comes and says that all of the classes are going to have to take some standardized tests, and if the test scores in Miss Twining's class weren't good, the class would be shut down. The children are scared. They haven't learned like everyone else. They haven't been sitting at desks doing work like their peers. How will they do? Will they all fail?

When the test scores come back, Miss Twining's class has far, far surpassed all of the other classes in the school. The class is saved, and a message has been given. Learning is about moving and discovering to see what works and what doesn't. If it doesn't work, determine why. What adjustments should be made?

The Learning Skills Continuum Approach is about developing brains and learners that are thinkers. This involves guided practice in trying, adjusting, training, and flexing until the most efficient ways to do a task are discovered, understood, and internalized. This is how new and lasting habits and behaviors are developed.

Age is not an obstacle.

Today I spoke to an adult who was inquiring about testing for himself. It reminded me again how important it is that parents and practitioners understand that learning challenges are not the result of not being smart enough, and can be permanently corrected by understanding and addressing the culprit skills on the Learning Skills Continuum.

Sam is in his forties. He shared that he was always a poor student, and for most of his life, thought he was not bright. After years of carrying around the burden of, "Maybe I'm not smart enough," he decided to get some IQ testing done. He found out that he had a high average intelligence test score.

Even with the assurance that he's smart enough, Sam still second guesses himself and his abilities all of the time. Maybe his dysfunctional family and moving around so much in childhood was the reason reading was so hard. Maybe it was just his lack of confidence.

Reading and spelling have always been a struggle, and even though it's faster and better than it was, he has a fear of spelling and is embarrassed by mispronouncing words and leaving out or misspelling words in e-mails at work. Sam says that he likes to read, but it's always a pain, and he never finishes. "I don't know why," he reflects. Sam said that he never learned how to sound out words, so when he sees a name or new word when reading, his "anxiety meter goes up."

Sam shared that he had the IQ testing because he kept thinking he might be stupid. Now he wants further testing to see if there's a reason why he has always struggled with reading. "I want to know I'm not insane."

There are real, definable reasons why children and adults struggle with learning. They can be identified and corrected. The Learning Skills Continuum Approach helps us to do that.

Action items. . .
- Go to www.LearningDisability.com.
  Under "Free Articles," read:
  * "It's time to Change the Future for Students with Learning and Attention Challenges."

Core Learning Skills Training

*Using movement to build a foundation for
attention and learning*

In this chapter. . .

- Why tutoring and other methods designed to improve school success won't be effective until the core skills are developed
- How children and adults alike benefit from retraining through movement
- Why many behavior and academic problems seem to resolve themselves almost automatically when deficient core skills are corrected

Movement is critical to the ability to learn.

John Ratey, M.D., author of *A User's Guide to the Brain* says, "*Mounting evidence shows that movement is crucial to every other brain function, including memory, emotion, language and learning. Our 'higher' brain functions have evolved from movement and <u>still depend on it</u>.*"[1]

Learning gets its jump-start through the involuntary movements caused by the primitive survival reflexes babies are born with. There is a normal progression of movement activity that helps a child understand himself and accurately perceive and navigate his world. Interference, for whatever reason, to this normal development through movement can impact a child's attention, learning, interaction, and comfort in the world. We call these foundational movement patterns and skills core learning skills.

Retraining core learning skills can help learners of any age develop higher brain functions and mental control through movement. The 1994 film *Karate Kid* can help us understand this kind of training. In it, fifteen-year-old Daniel wants to learn karate. His mentor has him doing series of repetitive movements that seem to have nothing to do with karate. He paints the fence and waxes cars with very specific movements: "Wax on, wax off."

At the end of the movie, Daniel is in a difficult position with an adversary and to get out of it, has to use an extremely difficult karate move that he has seen but never done. It takes exceptional mental and physical control. Daniel is able to execute the move perfectly because all of the lower-level, repetitive movement training. He had created a solid, reliable foundation of skills that could support high levels of mental and physical control and flexibility. This is the premise behind Core Learning Skills Training.

Core Learning Skills Training is a program of movement and visual skills activities that integrates primitive reflexes, improves body and attention awareness and control, and develops visual skills, spatial orientation, and internal timing and organization.

Five primitive reflexes that are common stumbling blocks to easy learning are targeted in Core Learning Skills Training. Each reflex is worked on for four weeks, and longer if needed, in order to shutdown the automatic movement patterns and train higher levels of the brain to take control.

Along with the reflex integration exercises, a sequence of balance and movement activities is used to help the learner gain awareness and mental control over balance, breathing, eye movements, and coordinated body movements.

These are things that we tend to take for granted. After all, everyone can move. Why do we have to train skills as basic as crawling and walking? We see the symptoms of delays in these areas all the time. We just don't typically recognize them for what they are.

We see a person walking down the street and think, "Hmm, there's something unusual about that person. What is it?" The person may have an awkward way of walking because he swings one leg out slightly or moves the same arm and leg forward. Maybe he walks slightly forward on his toes. We may not spot exactly what it is, but we know there's something not exactly right.

Integrating primitive reflexes resolves multiple problems.

Second grader, Cloe, was very wiggly in her chair, hated tight clothing, and was very picky about foods. There were only five foods that she would eat. She had serious attention problems and was not coordinated in sports. Her arms and legs were a bit out of her control, making it look like she was "all over the place" when sitting or walking.

Cloe had learned to be sassy to get out of schoolwork, which was extremely challenging for her. Letters and words seemed to move around on the page when she tried to read, making her rebel even more. Cloe had low stamina, and as she got tired, her lack of attention and body control and her sassiness escalated.

As she went through her Core Learning Skills Training, Cloe began showing some remarkable changes. She started eating all different kinds of foods and seemed more comfortable in her own skin. She could wear all of the clothes in her closet, instead of just a few pieces that were loose or low on the waist. She was able to sit calmly and focus, keeping her arms and legs where they belonged. She quit standing out in a negative way in her classroom at school.

Who would have thought that Cloe's clothing and food choices were anything other than preferences and personality quirks? Or that her general disarray and constant movement were not Attention Deficit Hyperactivity Disorder?

Cloe had not developed good body awareness and mental control due to the interference of primitive reflexes. She was trying hard to compensate and exert control where she didn't really have it, which caused her to be in a constant high-alert state. This creates continuous stress on the immune system and drains energy reserves, causing fatigue and sensitivity.

Core Learning Skills Training was not going to teach Cloe to read, but it allowed her to gain mental control over her body, attention, and eyes so that she could sit, focus, and look at the page with greater ease. This allowed her to be more "available" and ready for reading instruction.

Core Learning Skills set the stage.

Core Learning Skills Training is for anyone struggling with life or learning because of retained primitive reflexes or poor attention or body control. Core Learning Skills Training involves some very elementary as well as some very fine levels of visual and motor control.

Because some of the movements are done on the floor, our first inclination when we brought this kind of training into the learning center was to use it only with young children. However, as we understood and could spot the ramifications of retained reflexes better, we realized that we couldn't exempt anyone from this training if they needed it, regardless of age.

We are convinced that this kind of training will have a life-changing impact, and even our older students have been willing to go for it. The results have been very rewarding. Students have become more integrated, "together" individuals, moving and functioning with greater ease in all areas because they are no longer fighting their bodies for control.

How do reflexes become integrated or inactive?

Infants make specific repetitive movements at first by reflex, but gradually by trial and error, and then by intentional control. In this process, the reflexes are integrated, and higher levels of thinking begin controlling muscle movement and planning sequences of movements. Reflex integration training uses similar repetitive movements. For example, the Moro or startle reflex causes a baby to fling his arms and legs out and throw his head back.

One of the movements used in Core Learning Skills Training is called the Starfish. The student sits at the edge of a chair and leans back, resting on the back of the chair. He lets his head drop back and spreads his arms open above his head and legs open with knees fairly straight and heels on the floor in a starfish-like position. Then he pulls everything in, bending forward with arms crossed over his chest, head tucked, and legs crossed. For added mental control, we often have students cross their right arm over left and right leg over left on the first repetition, then reverse it on the next.

Individuals who have retained the Moro Reflex may tend to hold themselves rigidly to counteract its effects. If your arms fling open every time your head goes back a little, you're going to find yourself knocking things over and hitting people accidentally. The child won't understand why this happens but may subconsciously learn to avoid it by keeping his neck and arms tense.

By doing the starfish movements repetitively, the student is consciously controlling the movements of his head and limbs. He is training his muscles to respond to his thinking as opposed to a reflex. At first, in the training, the child's neck may be very stiff and the movements jerky, but gradually, as the reflex begins to disappear, the movements will appear more relaxed and coordinated.

Life and learning are supposed to be easy.

The goal of Core Learning Skills Training is to help people learn to live in an easy way. Compensations mean the child is doing something in a complicated and less efficient way. For example, if a child does not have a good sense of right and left on herself, she may have to use clues every time she sees or wants to write a **b** or a **d**.

If a person is compensating for retained reflexes, he may have to hold himself very rigid to stay seated in his chair or not bump someone in line and get into trouble. Having to use cues for right and left and having to consciously keep the body in control means that the person is working too hard. It takes too much energy to learn and behave.

Integrating reflexes and training the brain and motor system for better control and learning involve using the frontal lobes of the brain, or the higher thinking, to shutdown the automatic motor pattern so the person can try a different way. This takes attention, awareness, visualization, and planning.

Using guiding questions to develop awareness

The therapist or parent's job in this process is to guide the student in making the movements, then through questioning, help him to become aware of how his body is working and what adjustments he might want to make.

We use questions to direct the child's attention to specific parts of his body and help him become aware of how the movement felt and how he could change it to gain more ease, flow, and control. Here are examples of this kind of questioning:

- Without looking down, can you tell if your knees are straight or bent? Can you make them even straighter?
- Would you say you were moving fast, medium, or slow? Could you do the same thing but even more slowly this time?
- Were your arms and legs moving together on the same side or opposite sides? How do we want them to move?
- (Arms crossed over chest) Think about how your arms are crossed. Which arm is on top? Which arm do you want to have on top?

This kind of questioning is valuable anytime you want your child to develop better awareness and control, and is much more effective than telling because it engages the child's conscious awareness and decision-making.

We use this kind of questioning not only for Core Learning Skills Training but also to support attention training, handwriting, reading rate and intonation, math, comprehension, expressive language and social skills. Questions can be used to guide and improve learning in virtually anything that requires the child to think about her response or performance and make some kind of adjustment to understand or improve it.

In Core Learning Skills Training, the aim is not to get the movement "right." We are not training a set of "normal" movements into the child. We are using movements to develop learning. Learning involves thinking, comparing, evaluating, planning, visualizing, adjusting, and ultimately finding the most effective ways to do things.

We are not interested in training in a "splinter" skill that the student can execute but not apply. We are looking to build mental flexibility. If I have learned something in one way, can I now do it in a different way? Can I choose to do it faster or slower? Can I do it if I start on a different foot? Can I do the pattern backwards or from a different starting point?

Children with learning and attention challenges are often very inflexible. They are disrupted by any change in routine. They have only one way of doing things because they do not have the physical and mental flexibility to feel secure trying something in a different way. The mental flexibility and adaptability needed for ease in learning, social relationships, and general functioning begins at the core learning skills level.

The five reflexes specifically worked on in Core Learning Skills Training are the Moro reflex, Tonic Labyrinthine Reflex (TLR), Spinal Galant, Asymmetrical Tonic Neck Reflex (ATNR), and Symmetrical Tonic Neck Reflex (STNR). These reflexes are particularly important in early development of movement and visual skills but can interfere with developing the skills needed to read, learn, and pay attention easily in school if they stay active longer than they should.

Releasing energy by relieving chronic "flight or fight" stress

Relaxation and calming activities are included in Core Learning Skills Training. Children with poor attention and body control operate in fight or flight or hyper-alert mode much of the time. Telling them to relax or calm down doesn't work if they don't first have a sense of what it feels like to be calm.

Will, whom we met in Chapter 10, always threw a ball with abrupt, jerky force that made it very difficult for anyone to catch. When coached to throw more softly, he complied willingly, except that his next throw was exactly the same, with exactly the same result. Will thought that he was throwing softer, but because he always carried so much tension in his muscles, he didn't know what it felt like to move in a more relaxed and controlled way. Awareness is the first step in making a change.

Relaxation and calming activities typically involve deep-breathing. Deep breathing immediately forces oxygen into the brain, which improves thinking and encourages muscles to relax as they are flooded with oxygen-rich blood.

One of the relaxation and calming activities that we find extremely effective for almost any age is the heart-breathing strategy[2] developed by *Heartmath®, LLC.* Here's how the technique might look if you were observing your child doing this in a session at our learning center:

The child is instructed to breathe in and out slowly, imagining the breath flowing around the area of his heart. The therapist watches the child breathe like this until she sees that he is visibly beginning to slow down his breathing and relax his facial muscles and body.

While continuing the heart breathing, the child will be guided to remember a time when he felt deeply appreciated or to imagine a place or event that makes him feel really happy and good. Genuine feelings of appreciation trigger a chemical reaction in the body that supports our immune system and a sense of calm and well-being.

Heart breathing is an excellent technique for reducing anxiety and controlling stress. It provides a strategy for consciously slowing down one's heart waves or heart rhythm, which also slows down brain waves to produce a calmer, clearer state for thinking, learning, emotional balance, and decision making. Through the heart breathing technique, children can learn to recognize what it feels like to be calm.

Applying this technique to homework time, test-taking, oral presentations, and emotional stresses gives children a tool for conquering some of the fears and frustrations they face. In the process of developing core learning skills, knowing what it feels like to relax the muscles and feel calm is a step toward body and attention control.

Building on a foundation of reflex integration and relaxation, higher levels of mental and physical control are developed through a series of balance activities and movements that improve understanding of left-right and top-bottom, and coordination between the two sides of the body.

Developing better balance to develop mental focus

Daredevils throughout history have stunned the public by walking across Niagara Falls on a tightrope. Can you imagine the amount of mental control it must have taken to balance so perfectly all the way across that 1,200-foot gap?

Core Learning Skills balancing activities require balancing on two feet, one foot, and while walking on a low balance beam. Though these "balancing acts" are not nearly as impressive (or dangerous!) as the Niagara Falls tightrope walkers, they serve to develop mental control over the body, emotions, and attention.

The one- and two-foot balance activities are done with the eyes open and then with the eyes closed. Learning to remain in control with the eyes focused in one place not only facilitates balance, but also improves attention and the ability to ignore distractions.

Balancing with the eyes closed means that the child must have an internal focal point. Ultimately, much of our thinking and planning occur only in our mind without physical rehearsal. Using an internal focal point moves the learner to an even higher level of mental control.

Cognitive or thinking activities such as computing math facts, orally spelling words, telling the meaning of vocabulary, or answering questions are added onto the balance activities to make sure the child can maintain balance and think at the same time. When the brain has to think about something besides the physical activity, the control over balance starts to become automatic. Automatic control of balance and movement frees up the brain for learning and communication.

A child will be sidetracked from learning whenever she has to expend mental or physical energy and attention on sitting up straight, sitting still, keeping her eyes in one place, or not losing her balance while standing or walking. Energy and attention to listen to the teacher, comprehend a reading passage, and connect in conversations and discussions are dramatically reduced. Learning should be easy and natural and not be full of struggle and effort.

Learning where they are in space helps children build internal organization.

Children with reading disabilities often struggle with spatial orientation, particularly with right and left. Similar letters such as b and d and n and u can be confusing. Understanding right and left and top and bottom for discriminating letters starts with having a sense of right and left and top and bottom on ourselves.

This is why understanding the learning skills continuum is so important. Working on correcting letter reversals (seeing or writing letters backwards) and inversions (turning letters upside down) in reading and writing is extremely difficult and often fruitless if the person does not have an internal sense of spatial orientation. One segment of Core Learning Skills Training deals specifically with building spatial sense and internal organization from inside out.

Vision and coordinated movement activities prepare students for success in sports and school.

Bilateral movement activities help students to coordinate the right and left sides of their body. Children who are clumsy and poor at sports often have challenges in this area. Through the training activities, students learn to intentionally use their limbs to move homolaterally, or one side at a time, and bilaterally, using opposite sides together.

This builds internal awareness of what it *feels* like to move awkwardly with homolateral movements, or smoothly in coordinated bilateral movements, while also building the mental flexibility to shift from one to another.

Strong visual skills are essential to comfortable and efficient learning. Development of visual skills is integrated throughout Core Learning Skills activities beginning with reflex integration activities. The eyes provide the anchor for balancing activities and the "steering wheel" for movement activities. Finer levels of visual control are worked on specifically to help the eyes work efficiently together and build the visual skills needed for reading and academic work.

Core Learning Skills Training produces dramatic and rapid changes.

Core Learning Skills Training consistently results in "more together, normal" kids, greater self-esteem, and more success at school. Here are some examples:

- Cloe no longer stands out in class and is now excelling in reading.
- Alec is no longer getting sick all the time.

- Jacob moves easily and in a coordinated way, instead of looking like a robot.
- Karrie is thinking and responding much faster.
- Micah can now write with legible handwriting and is no longer exhausted by written homework.
- Jared has made friends.

Helping babies develop core learning skills

Parents of infants and toddlers often ask what can be done at an early age to help their children develop core learning skills naturally. Here are some tips:

- Babies need tummy time when they are awake. This allows for movement opportunities and causes them to have to exert more effort to move their muscles and look around than if they are on their back or confined in a swing or infant seat. The effort to move is good at this stage, as it develops muscle tone, trial and error, and intentionality of movement.
- Toddlers and young children need lots of opportunities to run, jump, and explore. What looks like unstructured playtime is highly conducive to developing the motor and visual skills needed for learning.
- Get off the computer! Children will have a myriad of opportunities to use the computer in their growing up years. Using the computer involves fine muscle control and coordination of the hands and eyes that is not fully developed in young children. These important skills are built on a foundation of large motor movements and control that do not occur in front of a computer screen. They develop outside where children can experiment with various kinds of movements and use their eyes and bodies to perceive and learn about various heights, distances, and speeds.

Core Learning Skills Training addresses skills that are just that—core to every aspect of higher learning. Children who have not made the expected progress in tutoring and other therapies may very well have interference related to these lower-level motor and visual skills. This is an area that is often overlooked but which can have a profound impact on a child's school success and future.

Action items. . .

- Go to www.LearningDisability.com.
  Under "Free Articles," read:
    * "Let's Get Moving."
    * "The Lost Art of Questioning."

CHAPTER 16

Auditory Stimulation and Training

Why sound therapy and audio-vocal training are such powerful tools for retraining listening skills and improving learning, relationships, attention, language, and reading

In this chapter. . .

- Why listening is so important to effective learning
- The role of high and low frequencies in thinking and motor skills
- The far-reaching benefits of sound therapy in attention, relationships, balance and coordination, organization, and much more
- The critical role active listening exercises play in improving speaking, reading, and comprehension skills

Improvements can begin in the first weeks of therapy.
According to school records, thirteen-year-old Michelle was inattentive, easily distracted, excitable, impulsive, restless, and having a problem with attention span. She had inconsistent grades, ran with the "wrong" crowd, and had even cut school a few times. She was bright and friendly but did not accurately perceive much of the information she was hearing.

As a result, she tended to try to fill in what she thought was being said or what she thought she was supposed to do. This led to her making up stories and being labeled as a troublemaker.

Michelle's parents were concerned about her difficulty staying focused, comprehending, and retaining abstract concepts. They felt that she was not always accurate in her perception of herself and of the emotions of others. She played the blame game well and rarely took responsibility for problems that came up with peers or teachers. Michelle became confused in noisy situations, and as a result, she often seemed lost and unsure about what was really going on.

She had difficulties in comprehension, listening skills, and seeing the gestalt, or "big picture." She had very strong compensatory strategies. Michelle was able to act as if she "had it all together and everything was great," but she was really only getting little bits of what was going on. While she seemed very social and had high energy, social situations could be very overwhelming for her.

Michelle's performance on the Tomatis Listening Test[1] showed that her ears were functioning very differently. This kind of listening pattern makes it difficult for the individual to accurately conceptualize the world, as she perceives mixed messages from what she is hearing. This may cause emotional problems and confusion with language and social situations.

Michelle began a twenty-week program of Auditory Stimulation and Training (AST). This is a listening skills training program in which the student listens to specially recorded and prescribed classical music and nature sounds CDs at home and has auditory training lessons in the clinic three times a week.

At the beginning of her program, it was noted that Michelle was very inflexible with language. She did not recognize when something she read did not sound right and required a large amount of discussion to understand an author or speaker's intent. She tended to miss the obvious, so when she would try to understand something, she would not get the real point, but come away with a connection that might make sense but was not really relevant.

After one week of Auditory Stimulation and Training (AST), Michelle reported that she didn't like the music and it made her tired.

After two weeks of AST, Michelle's mom said that Michelle was feeling something but couldn't articulate it. She was more willing to listen. Her mom noticed that Michelle was more relaxed and not as tense and anxious. She started asking questions and articulated her difficulty with understanding vocabulary, both of which were very unusual for her. She was more expressive and initiated conversations with her Dad, which was extremely gratifying for her parents to see.

After four weeks of AST, Michelle's mom said that Michelle believed nothing had changed; however, her parents felt the changes were very dramatic. She was "full of questions, which she never was before because she didn't want to deal with the language."

Her mom said, "It is as though she has awakened from a long sleep. We can ask her to do things now that we haven't asked or tried to teach her before because it was just too much. It is as though she has been far away." Her parents said that she was happier, and more "there." She was less timid in conversations and "able to be the person she was intended to be."

In sessions, Michelle was quicker at making connections. She said that she could remember more things that her mom told her.

After six weeks of AST, Michelle told her parents that she hadn't changed; *they* had! Her parents said that they probably had changed since they were now able to deal with her differently.

After eight weeks of AST, Michelle's mother reported that even though Michelle had missed two weeks of listening due to being away at camp, she did not lose any of the changes that had occurred. Her parents again said that there was such a big difference in her. She was asking more questions and really interested in the answers.

Michelle had some social issues come up at camp, which had not been unusual in the past, but she was able to explain to the counselor what she was thinking and meaning, and took responsibility for her part in the problem. She had not been able to do this before. She expressed that she was getting a "fresh start." Her mom felt this was a big step for Michelle because she would not previously have believed that she *could* get a fresh start.

Throughout the remaining twelve weeks of Michelle's Auditory Stimulation and Training program, her parents reported continued steady improvement in her understanding. Her mom shared that Michelle had a great attitude in everything. School was much better both academically and socially. She was getting good grades. In mid-October, her mom reported that Michelle was getting an A-plus in History. The previous year, History had been her "absolute worst" subject.

In Michelle's learning process, one of the biggest changes her parents saw was in her ability to verbalize what she was thinking or how she was working through something. Before, she could never verbalize what or how she was doing something, so it was very difficult for her parents to figure out where or what the problem was (for example, on a math assignment or in a disagreement with a friend).

Michelle's mom said that emotionally, Michelle had had difficulty expressing herself in the past, so she made some bad choices and held in bad feelings. Now that she was able to express her feelings better, she did not seem to be making poor choices.

Comprehension skills in reading and listening continued to increase during the second half of the listening training when the focus was on immersing Michelle in grade-level reading. At first, she was focusing more on reading the words than on thinking about the meaning. She would read whole passages and not be able to tell what they were about.

However, each week, an improvement was noted in this. Michelle became much more able to summarize a variety of types of material. She still tended to be too literal at times, and did not always see the most obvious connections, but she was much more on target with her comprehension before any questioning or discussion. With discussion, she was more easily able to assimilate a different idea, new vocabulary, or a different interpretation. This showed important improvement in flexibility and comprehension.

As learners, we do not have to *know* everything, but we do need to be able to think about and work with information in order to acquire new understandings. This is something Michelle had great difficulty with when she started her auditory stimulation program. She showed exciting growth in this ability.

Michelle's parents said that she was no longer misinterpreting questions or requests as much. Her understanding of conversations and discussions improved, and as a result, she was more "present," less defensive, and a more appropriate and productive participant, both socially and at school.

The changes Michelle was able to make in her understanding, communication, and learning were the result of Samonas Sound Therapy, which improved her desire and ability to listen, and her specific audio-vocal training lessons on the microphone, which stimulated her ability to monitor and focus her communication.

An overview of Auditory Stimulation and Training

Auditory Stimulation and Training (AST) is a combination of Samonas Sound Therapy and directed audio-vocal training lessons. AST is most typically done as a twenty-week program but may be reduced or extended to meet the needs of individual students.

For the duration of AST, the student listens to prescribed Samonas Sound Therapy CDs for fifteen to thirty minutes daily. The listening protocol is developed to meet the target needs and goals of the individual child.

Samonas Sound Therapy is a highly specialized and exquisitely recorded series of classical music and nature sounds CDs that is used to improve auditory processing, coordination and organization, attention, listening and communication, thinking, and learning.

Sound therapy increases the brain's ability to pay attention to a wide range of frequencies in sound. The lower frequencies in sound are especially important for coordination, movement, rhythm, and organization. Mid-range frequencies are especially important for hearing and reproducing speech sounds.

High frequency sounds are energizing to the brain and are critical for attention, thinking, and learning. The high frequencies in sound also carry the detail information, which makes it possible to discriminate between similar speech sounds and words, tone of voice, and different instruments and voices.

People who frequently mispronounce words, have low energy, get confused or misunderstand when listening, or speak with poor inflection or a monotone voice typically have poor listening skills.

Once the brain is processing a greater range of frequencies in sound, the listener will have better energy and better input with which to think and learn.

Audio-vocal training is used throughout the majority of the AST program. The child uses either a headset or standing microphone to speak into during the lessons. The child's amplified voice and Samonas music can be heard through the headphones.

Audio-vocal training is used to help the person's voice acquire the wide range of frequencies that his brain is learning to hear or pay attention to. When the voice is richer and contains a wider range of frequencies, it becomes the ongoing stimulus for the auditory system. This has many positive outcomes:

1. Speaking now provides energy to the brain for thinking
2. The person is more interesting to listen to
3. Social and communication skills improve
4. The ability to hear one's voice more accurately allows the person to monitor her speaking and reading accuracy
5. Singing improves
6. The person is better able to monitor the content of what he says.

Understanding sound therapy

There are many sound therapy programs available today. Sound therapy uses classical music and nature sounds CDs that have been scientifically engineered to enhance certain frequencies in music and sound to stimulate the brain for better attention and listening.

If a person is processing a narrow range of frequencies in sound, she will not have accurate and complete information to think with. By increasing the contrast between the high and low frequencies, and by "highlighting" the high frequencies or detail sounds, the brain is alerted to pay attention.

Listening is intentional. There has to be a desire to listen. We don't always know why a person's auditory system is not efficient, but it can be related to difficult birth, ear infections, trauma, exposure to loud noises, and stress or overload. Many students with learning disabilities and other learning challenges have poor listening skills, or auditory processing.

Weak listening skills can become a vicious cycle. If the brain is not getting good information auditorily, the desire to listen will decline. Since there is a connection between the emotional part of the brain and the middle ear muscles, which are so instrumental in moving sound to the inner ear, the middle ear muscles may quit working as hard to listen.

Sound therapy exercises the middle ear muscles so they can send a stronger message, and stimulates the attention and emotional centers of the brain to increase the interest and desire to listen. It wakes up the brain to listening and energizes the cortex, or higher cognitive part of the brain, for thinking, learning, and communication.

Samonas Sound Therapy

We have found Samonas Sound Therapy to be a cornerstone in the success of our students. Samonas was developed by German Sound Engineer Ingo Steinbach. With his extensive background in physics, music, psychology, and engineering, he has combined the principals of music therapy with the research of Dr. Tomatis to create a highly effective sound therapy system that is gentle, powerful, and prescriptive.

In order to function and learn well, a person must have a strong sense of himself as a reference point from which to view the world. He must have a sense of where his is in space in relation to others and his environment. Spatial orientation affects a person's ability to organize and reorganize. It is critical to being able to associate or relate information to known spots. When we lose this, we become very scattered and disorganized. We may start things and not know how to end them. We may have trouble staying focused on task.

Samonas music is recorded live and in such a way that the listener experiences natural, three-dimensional space. Music can be prescribed to help the student improve her spatial orientation and sense of self as a reference point. We pair Samonas Sound Therapy with Core Learning Skills Training and Attention Focus Training to help students develop body and attention awareness and control.

Support for social skills

As we all know from watching movies, music touches us emotionally. Because Samonas Sound Therapy is prescriptive, we can use it specifically to help withdrawn students engage and to stimulate the brain for language, communication, and relationships.

Al was a nineteen-year-old college dropout when we met him. He was smart, athletic, and talented musically. He had always had some struggles in school, though not significant enough to get any extra help. He had trouble making friends and tended to be a loner, often feeling depressed. After two weeks on his Samonas Sound Therapy program, listening fifteen minutes twice a day to his prescribed CD, Al said, "I've always been up and down, mostly down. But now I'm mostly up!"

After four weeks, Al had ventured out and met new people. He was excited and amazed that he had actually made friends and that people seemed to like him. Al has since successfully gone back to college and says, "I'm a listener for life." The stimulation of Samonas has provided Al a drug-free way to improve and consistently support his energy, mood, and relational skills.

Energy, organization, and attention

Higher frequencies in sound help to energize the brain for thinking, attention, and learning. The combination of the higher frequencies and the rhythm and structure of the specific Samonas music selections helps students become organized for attention, handwriting, math, reading, oral and written expression, multitasking, higher thinking, and problem solving.

When Rafael was leaving to attend medical school in Mexico City, he expressed concern about his ongoing struggle with attention and his fear that he would not be able to keep up. We provided a Samonas Sound Therapy program for him. He reported to us by e-mail dramatic changes in his ability to maintain his alertness and focus in class. He was extremely excited by the ease and effectiveness of the program, which was helping him to keep up in the rigorous environment of medical school.

AST Reading, Language, and Comprehension

AST, or Auditory Stimulation and Training, combines passive listening (Samonas) with active listening training. Through the work of Alfred Tomatis, Paul Madaule, Gayle Moyers, and other listening therapists world-wide over the last fifty years, the importance of active listening through audio-vocal training has been shown repeatedly.

To get the most out of the training for each student, we target the audio-vocal lessons to each student's specific challenges.

This way, we can not only get the benefits of improving auditory processing, but we can build related skills at the same time.

AST-Reading is used for students whose primary difficulties, in addition to auditory processing, relate to decoding, reading, and spelling. Directed audio-vocal training lessons improve critical skills for listening, speaking, and reading.

Specific reading activities are integrated into the lessons to improve phonemic awareness (the ability to think about the sounds inside of words), visual attention to detail, and reading accuracy, fluency, and comprehension. Lessons on multisyllable processing and a variety of oral reading exercises help students to self-monitor and correct their word reading errors, intonation, and reading flow.

AST-Comprehension is used for students who may be able to read but have challenges with listening and reading comprehension. Audio-vocal training lessons specifically address the auditory skills needed for good listening and processing of auditory information. Critical underlying skills for comprehension are embedded into the lessons. These include:

1. Getting a clear message: accurate discrimination of sounds and syllables, auditory memory, "hearing" the flow and intonation of the language, and attention to detail.

2. Visualizing while listening or reading. (People who comprehend well "make a movie" in their head as they read or listen. It is not possible to remember every word that is heard or read, but if the language is stored as images, the content and meaning can be retained and remembered easily).

3. Understanding the gestalt, or whole idea of material heard or read and seeing how the details fit into the big picture.

4. Understanding the story grammar, or the key content elements in material that is read or heard. This encompasses the *who, what, when, where, why, how, problem,* and *resolution.*

5. Verbal reasoning: analyzing and answering inferential and evaluative questions, and verbal problem solving.

Children who have poor language skills for speaking and listening are placed in *AST-Language*, which focuses on stimulating the auditory system for clearer and more accurate processing of language for listening, speech, and communication. The audio-vocal training lessons develop phonemic awareness, articulation, vocabulary, and language competency through a carefully sequenced progression of expressive language skills.

Errors made by students in any of the AST programs are generally handled by having the instructor say exactly what the student said followed by what she wanted the student to say. This is much more effective than just having the student "try again," since the brain learns by contrast.

A child who mispronounces a word when repeating or reading may not be "hearing" or processing all of the sounds in the word. By saying what the student said and then saying the word the correct way, the brain can hear the difference, making it possible for the student to correct the error. This technique can be applied to difficulties with grammar, tone of voice, and reading rate and fluency. For example:

1. A person with auditory processing problems may use an abrasive tone of voice and not realize it. Telling the person to speak nicer doesn't mean anything if he can't "hear" how he sounds. When the instructor says the same words with an abrasive tone followed by a gentle tone, the listener can hear the contrast and make a change.
2. Students who read extremely fast, flying across punctuation, often cannot adjust their speed when told to slow down. However, if they hear the instructor read extremely fast and then at a clear moderate speed, they can process the difference and begin to make a change.

This important concept of contrast is very effective in auditory training but can be applied to other areas of learning as well.

We have been continuously astounded by the consistent and dramatic outcomes of auditory training including:

- Better articulation
- Improved sleep
- Better ability to follow directions
- Improved auditory comprehension
- Improved vocal quality
- Better organization
- Improved social interaction

- Increased balance and coordination
- Improved language
- Increased attention
- Improved communication
- Reduced sound sensitivity
- Increased frustration tolerance
- Increased reading and learning

Joshua's Story

Four-year-old Joshua didn't talk, at least not more than a word or two at a time. He always sat on the sidelines at preschool, observing but not participating. He didn't have any of the typical four-year-old's exuberance and playfulness, even with his family. Joshua's mother shared that he "struggled with simple tasks and became exceedingly frustrated when he was unable to communicate his needs and desires."

Language output is dependent upon good input. Joshua's use of language exploded once he started his listening program. His mother was an excellent observer and documenter of his progress. Here are her thoughts upon completion of his twenty-week program of Auditory Stimulation and Training:

"Unbelievable…amazing…miraculous are but a few words to describe Joshua's progress since starting Samonas Sound Therapy. Joshua no longer sits on the sidelines while others are playing. He participates in group activities. He also enjoys 'horseplay' with his dad and brothers. He's more aggressive with them now. He's extremely imaginative.

". . .He is now able to follow simple instructions without constant repeating. He still requires structure and routine but not as stringently. He is less frustrated because he is able to communicate his feelings to others. Joshua has also gained a sense of humor and a wonderful air of confidence."

Jarrett's Story

Jarrett came to the learning center as a 2nd grader. He had been diagnosed with apraxia, a sensory or motor impairment that affected his gross motor coordination, graphomotor skills (handwriting), and oral motor skills.

When he started, Jarrett showed extreme difficulty with any fine or gross motor movements, organization, or coordination. He had difficulty articulating sounds and words, often making his speech unintelligible. He had difficulty expressing himself in a way that others could understand.

Jarrett was obviously very bright but had problems with social and language comprehension. He had huge amounts of uncontrolled energy and serious attention problems. He could attend to a task for ten to fifteen minutes with re-direction. He was a non-reader, had trouble making friends, and had poor self-esteem.

After four weeks of AST, Jarrett had better control in swimming; more eye contact; clearer, more controlled language; and had begun asking questions about conversations and other things in general.

After six to seven weeks of AST, Jarrett was using larger words and more mature sentences and questions. His sentences were no longer fragmented, and his speech was much easier to understand. He showed dramatic improvement in artwork (from scribbles to drawings) and better motor coordination. He started doing front and back somersaults in the pool, with control. He wrote a note on his own for the first time and posted it on his bedroom door. He made two good friends! His self-esteem was reported as high.

At the end of Jarrett's twenty-week listening program, his learning skills had improved dramatically. His increased attention, motor coordination, articulation, communication, and auditory and language processing abilities allowed him to be ready for further processing skills development and academic skills.

By third grade, Jarrett's reading was at grade level, and his articulation and motor skills had improved to the point that his originally very appropriate diagnosis of apraxia was being challenged.

When Jarrett started his listening program, his drawings were scribbles. Here are sample drawings from six weeks, fourteen weeks, and sixteen weeks into his program that illustrate his changes in organization, awareness of detail, and motor control.

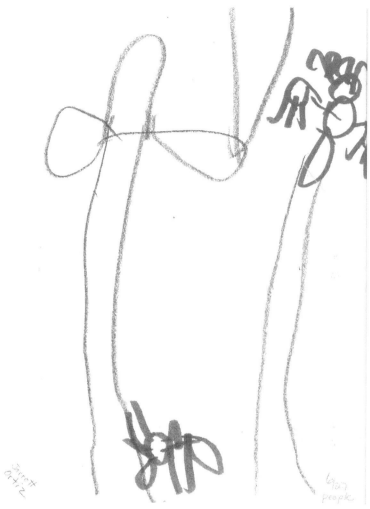

6 weeks: People

14 weeks: A map of a boat that he was
going to build out of Legos

16 weeks: The Earth and planets

Auditory Stimulation and Training spans may levels of the learning skills continuum. It supports development of core learning skills, auditory processing, memory and other processing skills, and basic academic skills. It may solve the learning challenges for a student, or it may be a step in the overall solution.

Action items. . .
- Go to www.LearningDisability.com.
  Under "Free Articles," read:
    * "Breakthroughs in Auditory Processing."
- Go to www.FixLearningSkills.com.
    * Listen to "Auditory Processing – Part 2."

CHAPTER 17

Processing Skills Development

How mental skills training can improve school performance

In this chapter. . .
- The tools a child needs to operate without wasting time or energy
- Why children typically enjoy this training
- How school and relationships change as the result of processing skills development

When smart children feel "dumb"

The participants introduced themselves at the beginning of the seminar about processing skills. When it was Leslie's turn, she said, "I am here because my son came home from school saying, 'I'm the dumbest kid in the class.' I have to find a way to help him."

Brett once felt like the dumbest kid in the class. He was smart but got all Ds in 5th grade. He got tired of trying hard and practically failing anyway, so he just quit caring, or at least he tried to make people think he didn't care. When he started his processing skills training with a program called PACE (Processing and Cognitive Enhancement), he was very resistant, but here are Brett's comments following his twelve-week program:

"[This] has helped me in math, reading, and all the rest. It has also made me be a better person. I am now a more thoughtful person. Before, I got bad grades. Now I improved in all subjects. My grades before were Ds. Now they have raised to As and Bs. It makes me feel special to be known as a smart kid. . ."

What are these skills that can turn a D student into an A and B student? When we look at any classroom, we see that not all learners are the same. You can have students with the same intelligence, from the same neighborhood, getting the same instruction, and one will finish the assignment in fifteen minutes and another may still be working on it after an hour. Why is that? It is because they come to the task with a different set of mental tools, or thinking skills.

Students need mental tools.

Just as a carpenter needs a set of tools to build with, students need a set of mental tools to think with. These include such things as:

- Memory – being able to take in enough information at a time and hold onto it long enough to store it or use it
- Attention – being able to focus on the important information and stick with it long enough to get it all
- Auditory processing – getting a clear and complete message when listening, and being able to process, or think about that information
- Visual processing – how we take in and understand information that we see
- Processing speed – how quickly we can take in, think about, and respond to information
- Executive function – a complex set of thinking skills that helps us organize and make decisions about information and behavior

Recent research on the brain and learning suggests that mental exercises can increase the connections between brain cells, making thinking and learning quicker and easier. The brain seems to work a lot like a muscle. The more you work it, the more it grows. Processing skills training is about exercising the brain. It is intense because intensity produces the quickest results, and it is motivating because children can see changes so rapidly.

Improving processing skills helps students to think and respond more quickly and accurately. The stronger a person's set of mental tools, the more efficiently and effectively he can do the job.

Unlike my son, who went off to college with a highly sophisticated laptop computer, I took a small, manual typewriter with me when I went away to school. Typing up reports was literally an all-night affair for me, as I had to retype the whole page every time I made an error (which was often). Computers are so forgiving that the same reports could now be typed and printed in a fraction of the time. The end product may be exactly the same, but the ease or difficulty of the route to get there is highly influenced by the tools used to do the job.

What happens in processing or cognitive skills training?

Processing skills training is generally done over a short period of time (ten to fifteen weeks). It is done five to six days a week, and the sessions are fun but intense. The students will do many different activities in a one-hour session. The activities may feel like drills or games but do not generally feel like schoolwork. They typically target one particular area of processing but have many other skills integrated into the activity.

In life, we never use just one mental skill in isolation, so this integration of skills is very important. For example, an activity may be primarily targeting visual memory but working on spatial orientation, concentration, and timing at the same time. Here are the keys to success in processing skills training:

- **Intensity** – The goal is to literally create new neuropathways in the brain. The way to make new and lasting connections in the brain is through intensive, repetitive training.
- **One-to-One** – Cognitive training will be most successful when provided on a one-to-one basis. This facilitates the necessary intensity and allows for tailoring the program to the individual student's needs. Janie, for example, is very good at reasoning but weak with memory skills. While she will work with both areas and many more in her program, a strong focus will be on memory. Cody, on the other hand, has good overall processing skills but slow processing speed and weak attention. He will use the same cognitive training program as Janie, but because the lessons are provided on

185

a one-to-one basis, increasing processing speed and extending attention will be emphasized in every lesson.

- **Immediate feedback** – We never want students to practice something incorrectly. In cognitive skills training, any error is immediately addressed, and the student gets the chance to do it again correctly. We want the brain to record the information correctly over many, many trials and do not ever want to breed confusion by allowing the student to rehearse something incorrectly.
- **Working at a challenging level** – The things that make the greatest change in the brain are those things that stretch us the most, so it is critical that activities be practiced at a challenging level.
- **Sequencing** – Levels within each activity should be sequenced in such a way as to build upon previous learning and continually but gradually add further challenge.
- **Loading** – The processing skills being trained, such as remembering, paying attention, visualizing, and thinking about the sounds in words need to be so automatic for the learner that they become a part of his thinking. This way, energy that is needed for learning is not having to be diverted into processing and remembering the information.

  Loading, or adding mental activities to the processing skills being trained, helps bring the skills to an automatic level. Mental activities include such things as computing math facts, answering questions, or carrying on a conversation while continuing to perform the processing skills task.

- **Adding distractions** – Adding distractions that the child has to deliberately ignore while doing the processing skills activities helps improve attention.

- **Self-monitoring of progress** – Research has shown that people perform better when they are able to monitor or track their own progress.
- **Variety of activities** – Having a variety of engaging activities keeps motivation and interest high for the learner and allows her to gain mental flexibility by training skills in many different ways.

Processing, or cognitive skills training, fits into the second and third levels of the Learning Skills Continuum. These are the areas of processing and executive function. Because the mental tools developed are universal to thinking, learning, and functioning, not only at school but at work and in the social arena as well, this kind of training has very broad applications.

Processing skills training will help students think faster and more effectively for the SAT and other college entrance exams. It will help athletes be more focused and integrated and quicker in their thinking and visual skills. It will help disorganized students to become more focused and aware. Students who are managing in school by the skin of their teeth will find themselves functioning better, with less effort, once their processing skills have been strengthened.

For the population of students with attention challenges or learning disabilities, this kind of training is a must. Once neurodevelopmental or core learning skills are in place, honing and integrating overall processing skills is the next step in creating a foundation for successful learning. The intensity of this kind of brain training helps increase attention, persistence, and willingness to move on after a mistake has been made.

Following processing skills training, most parents notice that their children are more independent with homework and are taking more initiative. Teachers typically report that they see an increase in the child's attention, task completion, and independence.

Confidence is almost always an outcome of processing skills training. Poor skills in any area related to memory, attention, auditory or visual processing, processing speed, or reasoning leaves a person with incomplete, inaccurate, or confusing information to think with. This creates insecurity and uncertainty at some level.

Improving processing skills and the speed and efficiency of thinking makes the world feel clearer and more secure. With better information with which to think and respond, children naturally gain confidence in their abilities and performance.

Processing skills training does not automatically teach a student to read, spell, write, or do math. If these basic skills were there but not easily accessed, students with a history of inconsistent performance will very likely blossom academically following cognitive training. Their stronger, more integrated and organized set of mental tools will allow them to retrieve, integrate, and use what they previously learned.

For some students, weak underlying skills have interfered to the point that they have been unable to understand and retain the basic skills in certain academic areas. In spite of hard work and special help from school, parents, and tutoring, reading or other academic areas have not clicked.

These students will need specific reading, spelling, writing, or math development following their cognitive training, but this time it will make sense and stick. Academic remediation goes much faster and works much better once the supporting skills are in place.

Strong processing skills help students adapt to change.

Confidence, sense of security, and quality of life are a function of mental flexibility. The more flexible a person is, the greater the range of possibilities he can see. Mental flexibility is needed to solve problems and to adapt quickly and easily to change.

Donny loves assembly days at school because he likes the change of pace. He can easily adjust to having a longer than normal language arts period before recess because he can mentally process how the whole morning will go, in spite of the changes. He is excited about the assembly content.

Ben, who is in the same class as Donny, is very inflexible mentally. Any change is upsetting to him because he can't predict what will happen, and it makes him feel scared. He gets angry that the language arts period is extra long and refuses to do his work.

He doesn't want to leave the room to go to the assembly because it's supposed to be math time. Even though he doesn't really like math, he knows what to expect. He'd rather stick with what's familiar than deal with something unknown like an assembly, even though his teacher says it will be fun.

Ben has weaknesses in several processing skills areas, making it difficult for him to quickly and accurately assimilate information and understand the ramifications. He can't trust what he doesn't understand. Strengthening Ben's processing skills will help him to get the big picture more easily and adapt to change more comfortably.

Weak processing skills can cost the child time, energy, and effort.

Processing skills training always works toward the student doing things in the most efficient way. There are many ways to do things, but some ways take more energy, time, or effort. To move through school and life comfortably and independently, we want to do things in the most efficient way without wasting excess effort and energy. The following are some examples from our processing skills training programs.

Many activities require that the student respond to the beat of a metronome. This builds internal timing, attention, and quick decision-making. If the student is tapping her hand or bouncing her body in time to the beat as she is responding, she is using more physical energy and working less efficiently than if the beat were internalized and she were responding with only her voice.

In activities where the student has to move his eyes back and forth between two columns of letters and call out the sounds, moving only the eyes versus moving the head back and forth will be the most efficient way to do the task. When applied beyond the scope of cognitive training, an efficient reader moves only his eyes, not his head, as he reads across a line of text.

Playing cards are used in some activities. Because the tasks are challenging, children sometimes start out by placing their cards on the table so they can easily see and sort through them. Ultimately, they need to be able to do the task while holding and manipulating the cards in their hands if they are going to work in the most efficient way. After all, what poker player would ever dream of laying all his cards out on the table for everyone to see while he contemplates his next play?

Three cognitive training programs[1] that we have found to be highly successful with students are:

- PACE (Processing and Cognitive Enhancement), developed by Ken Gibson, D.O. and Learning Rx, Inc.
- Brain Spark, developed by developmental optometrist, Douglas Stephey, D.O., and
- Brainware Safari®, developed by Learning Enhancement Corporation.

All three of the programs train a wide number of processing skills critical to learning. They include all of the keys to training detailed above. They are highly engaging, intensive, well-sequenced, and provided on a one-to-one basis.

Attention skills, processing speed, and mental flexibility are built throughout these programs. All can be used very successfully with students ages six and up. PACE and Brain Spark are provided to students through direct instruction, from one trainer to one student. Brainware Safari® is a colorful and fun computer-based program with a video-game format.

Action items. . .
- Go to www.LearningDisability.com.
  Under "Free Articles," read
    * "Mental Boot Camp."
- Go to www.FixLearningSkills.com.
    * Listen to "Processing Skills."

CHAPTER 18

Attention Focus Training

What are the key principles in attention focus training that make it work and stick?

In this chapter. . .

- The many ways lack of focus is revealed in a child's behavior
- How children improve when they internalize the "feeling" of focus
- How simple methods and movements can help children learn to refocus on their own

Children are unaware of their inattention.

Ryan is looking around the classroom instead of doing his work. His teacher says, for the fourth time in twenty minutes, "Ryan, pay attention." Ryan looks up at her innocently and says, for the fourth time in twenty minutes, "I am."

Children with attention challenges, more often than not, aren't aware that they've lost their attention. They don't recognize their own symptoms of distractibility, impulsivity, or loss of focus that are so obvious to others. We once worked with a nine-year-old boy who would get up in the middle of class and begin walking around the room humming. He had no idea that he was doing it.

Heather was a beautiful, friendly twelve-year-old with extreme attention challenges. She was so distractible that she would literally flit from object to object and place to place within the room while carrying on a conversation or engaged in a lesson. She did the same thing when she was speaking. She spoke rapidly and switched topics so quickly it would make your head spin. She interrupted virtually every sentence she began with her next thought, which was often completely unrelated. And she had no idea she was doing it!

C.J. would get started on his work right away, but shortly after writing his name on the paper, his attention would drift and he would completely lose track of time. He was forever complaining that his teacher didn't give them enough time to do the work because he was so unaware of the time lost along with his focus.

When working with children who have attention challenges, it is important to recognize that their lack of attention is outside of their control. If they could pay attention easily and well, they would. Students are typically not aware that they have lost their focus, which makes it virtually impossible for them to correct it.

Attention focus training helps build awareness and control.

Attention focus training can help people of all ages develop an awareness of their particular kind of attention challenge and learn strategies for controlling it. Whether medication, diet, nutritional supplements, neurofeedback, or counseling are being used to treat the attention problems, attention focus training should be a part of the intervention. It provides a level of understanding and control that enhances all other therapies and cannot be attained in other ways.

Attention focus training is not about making kids pay attention. Children with attention deficits hear an endless stream of "pay attentions" from the adults in their life. They are often placed strategically in classrooms in order to be near the teacher so she can help keep them on target. Parents have learned to get eye-to-eye with their attention-challenged children to make sure that their instructions are heard. These strategies use external forces to control a child's attention. The goal of attention focus training is for the child to develop the internal awareness and control over his attention that will allow him to function independently and optimally.

There are four steps in the process of helping children develop attention awareness and control. Students must learn to:

1. Recognize what it *feels* like to be focused and what it *feels* like when they're not
2. Recognize what they *do* when they lose their focus

3. Recognize what caused the loss of attention
4. Choose a strategy for getting back "on" or regaining their focus

Step 1: Recognizing what it *feels* like to be focused or not

Imagine a ballet dancer, a tightrope walker, a surfer riding a wave all the way to shore, or a skateboarder smoothly handling the dips and curves of a skateboard park. What do these athletes have in common? They are highly focused and exquisitely balanced.

At the learning center, our first step in attention focus training almost always involves some kind of movement activity that allows the student to gain, maintain, and *feel* a sense of balance and control.

Let's use walking on a low balance beam as an example. (This could also be a curb or a tape-line on the floor). Students with attention challenges very often start walking on the beam in a fast, haphazard manner, wobbling and working hard to keep their feet on the beam. The therapist talks to the student in a low, slow, quiet voice, coaching her to walk slowly, to relax her shoulders and arms, to breathe slowly and begin to feel control.

We call this a kinesthetic voice. If we want a person to feel something physically or emotionally (in this case, calm, relaxed control of muscles, balance, and speed), we use a kinesthetic voice because the brain responds to a low, slow vocal rate and pitch by *feeling*.

Learning to gain and maintain the balanced and controlled feeling takes time for the student to develop, but in each session, as a change is noted, even if it is incremental, the therapist has the student step down from the beam, close his eyes, and breathe slowly.

Then the therapist coaches the student to remember the focused, controlled feeling that he had when he was walking on the balance beam. This is what it *feels* like to be focused. The child is instructed to open his eyes and discuss how it *felt* different to be focused and not focused when walking.

Step 2: Recognizing what they *do* when they lose their focus

What are the symptoms of the attention loss? What does the teacher, parent, or therapist see that tells them that the student has lost his attention? Does the child stare into space, pencil suspended over his paper? Does he start writing or speaking more rapidly or slowly? Does he start making more mistakes? Recognizing exactly what he does becomes a signal for the student that he has lost his attention so that he can do something about it.

Telling a student what she does when she loses her focus does not automatically mean she will be able to recognize the behavior from then on. It takes training through questioning. When Sasha loses her focus while listening or doing written work, she stares into space as though she is daydreaming. Helping Sasha recognize this behavior might look like this during a session:

Therapist: "What are your eyes looking at right now?"

Sasha: "Nothing."

Therapist: "Where should your eyes be looking?"

Sasha: "At my paper."

Therapist: "How do you think I knew that you had lost your focus?"

Sasha: "I was staring at the wall."

Therapist: "Try looking at your paper. Notice what is on it. Now stare at the wall but let your eyes 'look at nothing.' How does it feel different to look at your paper and to look at nothing?"

Sasha: "When I stare at the wall, my eyes feel kind of hazy."

Therapist: "OK, so whenever your eyes get that 'hazy' feeling, that's your signal to check your attention."

From this point on, whenever Sasha is staring blankly, the therapist will stop her and say, "Why do you think I stopped you?" or "You need to check your attention. What did I see that helped me to know that?" The therapist will keep dialoguing what the symptomatic behavior feels like so that the student can eventually recognize it herself, then challenge the student to stop herself and say, "I can tell I've lost my focus because I'm staring at the wall," before the therapist calls it to her attention.

Step 3: Recognizing what caused the loss of focus

Challenges with learning anywhere on the Learning Skills Continuum will stress the attention system. Confusion created by poor auditory or visual processing will trigger attention loss.

Matt, for example, had extremely poor phonemic awareness. He simply could not make sense out of the sounds in words. As a result, he was virtually a non-reader at seven years old. But he was very friendly and imaginative. Whenever Matt had to do reading or writing tasks in class, he would quickly lose his attention and talk to nearby classmates or find other ways to entertain himself. Telling him to pay attention and do his work had no effect other than to make Matt add "getting into trouble" to his repertoire of failures.

It is natural for people to lose attention when whatever they are working on makes no sense and creates confusion. Until Matt's phonemic awareness was developed so that he could learn and use phonics successfully, he was never going to be able to pay attention to reading and writing tasks.

Poor posture and body control due to weak core learning skills will divert attention. These challenges must be identified and corrected. As we saw with Chris in Chapter 7, demanding, or even working on training attention without addressing the underlying cause will be a losing battle.

Some students can focus but are easily distracted, and once their attention shifts, it stays there until something else more interesting grabs hold of it. This is the child who turns to look at the person walking past the open door of the classroom, and then continues to stare out the door even though the person is gone. He's losing time, but is probably not even aware of it until his teacher tells him to turn around and do his work.

Eleven-year-old Hector had his therapy sessions in a room that was divided into two work stations by a tall room divider. When the student on the other side of the divider began using a metronome (a device that makes a clicking sound to a given beat) Hector became quite agitated. He could not focus because he didn't know what the clicking was. We took Hector over to the other side of the room to see what was making the sound. He got to ask the other student what he was using the metronome for.

Then we taught Hector to say to himself, "I know what that clicking sound is. I don't have to pay attention to it anymore." We practiced over the next few sessions, alerting Hector that sometime during his session, he would hear that noise. His job was to identify what it was and then consciously tell himself he did not have to listen to it anymore. As Hector became proficient with choosing not to listen to the metronome, we began to apply what he had learned to distracting noises in his classroom, such as the pencil sharpener and other children talking.

Sandi's challenge with attention was completely different than Hector's. Sandi was a bright second grader in a private school who had good academic skills but whose response time was so slow that she was never able to complete her class work. She was always turning in partially completely papers, and because she worked so slowly, it was easy for her to lose track of what she was doing and make what looked like "careless errors."

Correcting the underlying problem causing Sandi's attention challenge had three facets. First was having her biochemistry evaluated, which led to eliminating dairy and sugar from her diet—huge culprits in slow response time. Second was specific training with the PACE program to improve processing speed, and third was attention training, aimed at helping Sandi recognize and adjust her working speed and response time.

Step 4: Choosing a strategy for getting back "on" or regaining focus

Once students can recognize that they have lost their attention, they have to have a strategy for getting themselves refocused. For Hector, in the example above, it was a matter of giving himself permission to stop paying attention to something once he had identified what it was.

Many students learn to pair the "focused, ready feeling" with a slow breath and thinking about an X. In the process of learning to recognize what it feels like to be focused, and to consciously get focused, we typically use balance and movement activities. Once the student can gain balance and control physically, he will also have increased his attention.

Students are taught to anchor that focused feeling by stopping the movement activity, closing their eyes, visualizing an X, taking slow deep breaths, and remembering the feeling of balance and control. We tell them that this is what it feels like to be focused.

When they are in their sessions, at school, playing sports, or doing homework, they can remember and access the focused, ready feeling by thinking about an X and taking slow, deep breaths. With practice, students of all ages become very proficient at using this "anchor" to regain their attention focus.

Strategies for use with attention training

Having a number of different approaches to choose from is very helpful in being able to match the strategy with the individual student. Suggested methods include **Brain Gym®** from the Educational Kinesiology Foundation, the **Vestibular Integration Sequence** detailed in Dr. Joan Smith's book, *You Don't Have to Be Dyslexic*, Dr. Deborah Sunbeck's **Infinity Walk**, and the **Learning Breakthrough** program by Dr. Frank Belgau.[1] All provide balance and movement activities that can be used to help students learn to recognize what it feels like to be focused and subsequently anchor and apply the focused feeling.

The Vestibular Integration Sequence involves walking and doing certain activities on a low balance beam. This requires slow, controlled movements and is an excellent match for the student who tends to be too speedy, as many of our attention-challenged children are. This is the student who moves too fast, talks too fast and probably too much, and rushes through his work. This student needs to experience the feeling of slowing down and moving with control.

A slow, lethargic student needs a technique that is more energizing, so Brain Gym® or the Learning Breakthrough Program might be used to energize the student and help him notice the increase in focus that accompanies his increased energy.

Students who have difficulty transitioning or whose attention is challenged by anger or frustration will be able to let go of the emotional overlay and become more "together" or integrated, calm, and focused using Brain Gym® or Infinity Walk techniques.

Two other techniques that we use often to assist in attention training are the Heartmath® breathing technique, described in Chapter 15, and Ron Davis' alignment strategy.[2]

The Heartmath® breathing strategy is especially helpful when anxiety is the root or a symptom of the student's loss of attention. This technique helps students recognize what it feels like to be calm and focused through controlling their heart rhythms. Once they become independent with the technique they have this tool easily available to use at any time to regain their confidence and focus.

Ron Davis, author of *The Gift of Dyslexia* and *The Gift of Learning*, discovered that dyslexic students often experience disorientation triggered by confusion about letters, punctuation, and small common sight words such as *the, of* and *if*.[3] Many dyslexic thinkers have an exceptional ability to visualize ideas and things three-dimensionally, but are confused by two-dimensional symbols such as letters and numbers.

Small words can be confusing in context because they do not create a strong mental image. If you see the word **cat**, you can easily picture what it is, but what is a **the**? When the dyslexic learner cannot attach meaning to what she is seeing, it can trigger disorientation and some of the dyslexic symptoms people typically think of, such as letters and words moving on the page.

I once had an adult dyslexic student tell me that punctuation marks were like gnats on the page. They didn't have any meaning for him, so they just tended to get in his way and cause him confusion and disorientation.

Disorientation is a specific kind of attention loss usually associated with reading or writing but which can also occur when listening. When a person is disoriented, it is like his brain is telling him something different than what his senses are telling him. In the case of a dyslexic reader, letters and words aren't really running off the page, but it may look and feel like they are.

Imagine you are in your car, stopped at a stoplight. A large truck next to you begins to move forward slowly, and you slam on your breaks. Has this ever happened to you? You reacted as though you were moving but you really weren't. You experienced disorientation. Your brain perceived something different than what your senses actually saw and felt.

The Davis alignment technique, which provides students a specific, visualized focal point, has been very effective as an attention-training tool for students who experience disorientation. Infinity Walk is also effective in helping control this kind of attention challenge.

Using attention skills any place, any time

Any new piece of learning needs practice in order to become automatic. Paying attention is a skill, not just something to be assumed. Attention training and practice using the new skills is a very important part of students' sessions.

Transferring the skills outside of the clinical setting is the next crucial step, as attention skills are only valuable if they can be used any time and any place. Students are guided in setting goals for when, where, and how they will try out their new skills. They visualize, role-play, and talk through exactly what they will do, think, and say to themselves. On their next session, we check in to see how it worked, adjusting and continuing this process until the attention skills become automatic in the student's daily life.

Tips for parents and teachers

Students with learning and attention challenges work harder than their peers to do the same task. There comes a point where their effort becomes counterproductive. When students are clearly showing signs of inattention—daydreaming, wiggling, impulsiveness, distractibility, and whining—it's time for a break. Here are some suggested Brain Breaks that take just a few minutes and can revive and refocus students:

1. Drink water (not tea, soda, juice, etc.) The human body is an electrical system. Water is needed to conduct electricity, and the brain is the first organ to dehydrate. Drinking water can perk up a wilted learner!

2. Move! Do Brain Gym® activities or Infinity Walk. Run around the block, do some push-ups, or shoot some baskets.

A brief movement break will re-energize the learner and allow for better focus.

3. Have a protein snack to provide energy for the brain.

Using a timer can be very effective in helping students improve their productivity. Determine how long the student can focus well on the particular task. This may be thirty minutes, or it may be five minutes. Choose an amount of time appropriate to the child and challenge him to complete a certain amount before the timer goes off. Make it feel like a contest and celebrate what the child was able to do in the given amount of time. Set the timer again and see if he can accomplish even more.

Classical music in the background or on headphones can be very focusing and organizing for children when they are working on class work or homework. Samonas Sound Therapy speaker CDs or Advanced Brain Technologies Sound Health® Series CDs are particularly effective for stimulating organization, focus, creativity, and learning and are easy to use in a classroom.

Most students with attention challenges respond extremely well to attention focus training. In fact, providing training for attention is a real gift to these learners, as it empowers them to be in control of their own attention, instead of having to have someone else constantly refocusing them so they can learn and behave.

Action items. . .
- Go to www.LearningDisability.com.
    Under "Free Articles," read:
    "More Time to Teach . . . More Motivated to Try."

Executive Function

Helping children take charge of their lives by developing their internal CEO

In this chapter...
- How inner language affects behavior
- Creating order out of disorder in a child's thinking and environment
- Valuable tips for stress-free homework

How a child learns to self-manage

"You're not the boss of me!" Rachel yells at her brother. This is a typical interaction between young siblings, but reflective of what normally developing children eventually want: to be in charge of themselves, to make their own decisions, and to manage their own lives. What are the skills needed for people to successfully be the boss of themselves?

- Verbal inner language
- Visualization
- Time orientation, sequencing, and management
- Ability to understand and manage space and materials
- Awareness of behavior and consequences (real life cause and effect)
- Use of strategies to plan and guide behavior
- Reasoning and problem solving
- Organized thinking (seeing categories, relationships, how multiple tasks or task components connect, and application of information)
- Mental flexibility

- Ability to see things from other perspectives and see other points of view
- Attention
- Language expression

These skills support the *executive* function of human thinking that allows us to evaluate information, strategize, make decisions, and follow through with a course of action. Once action is taken, our executive function evaluates the outcome and determines if this is an action, behavior, or response that should be repeated; and if not, what should be done instead. This high-level function of the brain is absolutely crucial to managing in a well-balanced, appropriate, and successful manner in life.

Executive function and the teenage brain

Executive function develops and becomes more sophisticated throughout childhood, the teenage years, and into adulthood. Adolescents and teens perceive themselves as being ready to take on the world on their own, but in reality, their executive function is usually not developed enough to fully support them in those tumultuous years of growth.

This is where much of the natural parent-teen conflict enters the picture. Parents who recognize their teen's blossoming competence and independence and find ways to foster it while subtly providing the advice and structure needed to keep them safe, usually get their children to adulthood fairly unscathed.

The real challenge occurs with children and teens that lag behind in their development of executive function. Parents of these young people are forced to be much more vigilant and active in organizing, structuring, and guiding their children's behavior and choices while the children are still experiencing the normal desire to be out from under their parents' thumb.

The good news is that the brain is malleable, and skills that haven't developed as efficiently as expected on their own can be developed through specific and intensive training.

The importance of using our inner voice

Inner language is the voice in our head that we use to work through problems and guide and evaluate our behavior. Training inner language skills involves developing an awareness of inner language, rehearsal, and conscious application of self-talk. To develop inner language, a child's therapist may do activities or games in which he will say something, such as a series of numbers, letters, words, or a line of a poem or rhyme and have the student "hear" the therapist's voice saying it again in her mind.

The therapist may coach the child to mentally "hear" the stimulus in a funny voice, a loud voice, or a whisper. The child may be challenged to hear part of it soft and part loud, or "listen" to it with one ear, then the other. Rhythm patterns can also be used in this kind of exercise. Playing with the auditory image helps students develop an awareness of their inner language and greater flexibility and control in using it. Inner language is used to facilitate attention control and many other aspects of training with executive function.

With attention training, use of inner language to refocus might look like this: The student is sitting in class. Someone in the back of the room begins sharpening a pencil. The student hears the noise, but before turning around, which would be his typical reaction, he says to himself with his inner language, "I know what that sound is. It's the pencil sharpener. I don't have to pay attention to that anymore." Application of inner language skills should be rehearsed through practice and role-playing exercises.

Words are very powerful. Words alone can trigger chemical responses in the body that can support or harm us. What people say to themselves with their inner language can be encouraging and uplifting or emotionally battering and draining. When the person is listening to an inner dialogue that says, "I'm so stupid. I always get these kinds of questions wrong. Everyone is going to make fun of me if I'm the last one done on the test," he is diverting mental attention away from the test questions and pulling down his confidence and energy.

At our center, we teach children to use their inner language as a tool to support energized, healthy, productive thinking and reactions. A child can change his response, and likely his performance on the test, by learning to take slow calming breaths before entering the classroom, and say to himself, "I do my best on tests when I read each question carefully and take my time."

Visualization is another form of inner language.

Visualization is visual inner language. The ability to automatically and easily create mental pictures of what is heard or read is a critical factor in comprehension. Visual inner language helps people organize their thinking by mentally seeing and manipulating the components such as different ideas, parts of a task, events in a week, how numbers should be aligned in a math problem, and relationships between people in a conversation.

To train visualization, we have children look up slightly and create an imaginary screen in front of them. People naturally look up when visualizing, so specifically guiding children to look up helps to trigger visual thinking. Having an imaginary screen to put the images on helps make them more concrete.

Visualization is trained through guiding questions that help the student make "pictures" in his imagination. This can start with looking at a picture, then looking up and making a mental image of it. A therapist will have the student point to and describe the things he remembers from the picture. Visualizing symbols, which is important for spelling, sight word development, mental math, and memorizing dates and complex graphics (such as the Periodic Table of Elements) can be learned.

The therapist will show the child the symbols. Then the child will be asked to look up, imagine, and point to them on her screen. She should simultaneously tell about what she is picturing to further strengthen the image and process it both visually and auditorily.

From picture imaging, the therapist guides the student in creating clear, accurate images that exactly reflect the intent of her words, phrases, sentences, paragraphs, and passages. If children say that they cannot make mental pictures, the therapist can make the process feel more real by saying something like, "If you were going to *draw* a picture, *who* would be in it? *What* would she be doing? *Where* is she? *What* should be happening in your picture?"

The visual system is very quick. It can handle a great deal of information at one time. The eyes naturally go up when visualizing, and a person's voice and gestures naturally get faster and higher when describing things that he is seeing. Knowing this, a therapist can use a quick, higher pitched "visual" voice and rapid, high gestures to help the student get into visual mode.

Visualization is an excellent tool for mental rehearsal. When Sal was getting ready to go into junior high school, he was very nervous about being able to find his classes. He was afraid he would get lost and be tardy. His mom took him to visit the school and walk from class to class to get the lay of the land. At home, his mom helped him mentally walk and talk his way from class to class again several times before the first day of school so that Sal would easily be able to navigate his way around.

The role of visual and verbal inner language in developing executive function

Both visual and verbal inner language are used throughout the process of learning to manage time, space, and materials. Getting places on time, completing things in a timely manner, and planning out a project or schedule requires an understanding of time.

How much time is a minute? What does it feel like? What can be done in a minute versus five minutes or an hour? How long do common daily tasks really take? How long do different kinds of homework assignments take?

Development of time management and planning begins with making sure the child is truly oriented in time, understanding the passing of time, relationships in time (for example the relationship between a week and a month), and sequencing.

There is nothing so frustrating to parents as their child coming home day after day without the materials needed to do his homework. Even more perplexing is the student who does his work and then loses it in the black hole of his backpack before ever turning it in. Students are given planners at school but often fail to use them, in spite of constant reminders.

I once had a high school student who perpetually (and unfairly) got Fs on assignments because he put his name on the left side of the page instead of the right. These difficulties that look so much like laziness or lack of attention or motivation may be symptoms of poor understanding of space and visual organization. These students do not automatically see how things are organized in space so they don't use drawers, closets, or organizers in notebooks or planners logically. They don't see the organization and logical placement of information on charts, graphs, math problems, or written papers.

Before the tools of organization can be used successfully, space must be explored and dialogued so that students understand why things are designed or placed where they are. Space should be explored from large to small. Think house, bedroom, closet, hanger. On a weekly planner, notice that the page shows a whole week divided into days, with each day divided into sections by hour. Are these things obvious? Yes. Are they obvious to everyone? No. And if they're not, organizing within that space will elude the student.

Instilling a sense of order

One of the methods that we have found at our center to be particularly effective is to help children explore space using the concept of order as opposed to disorder.[1] Order means "things in their proper place, proper position, and proper condition." Let's take a cup of coffee, for example. Its proper *place* might be in front of and slightly to the right of the person it belongs to. Its proper *position* is upright as opposed to upside down, and its proper *condition* is full of fresh, hot coffee.

We explore the meaning of order, as opposed to disorder, with the student using many real life examples that are meaningful to her. Then, using Ron Davis' concept mastery technique detailed in *The Gift of Learning*[2], we have the student build something, three-dimensionally with clay to illustrate the concept of order.

The child has to explain how her sculpture shows order. If the student built a bicycle in clay, she might say, "The tires show order because they are in their proper place, which is one on the front and one on the back. They are in the proper position, which is facing forward and not sideways, and they are in their proper condition because they are filled with air and not flat."

Once the student understands the concept of order and can show and verbalize the components, it can be applied to organization in math, on the page, with an assignment calendar, with materials in a backpack, to cleaning a room, or even to behavior.

Stan was an extremely bright eleven-year-old with overwhelming attention challenges. When he first started coming to his sessions at the learning center he was literally all over the place. He would bounce through the waiting room, open the doors of people's work stations, run through the center, and crawl under chairs. Once, when I came out to get him, he was in a chair upside down! His head was on the seat and his feet and bottom were up in the air.

We worked with Stan on the concept of order. Then we began to apply it to everything in his life. He learned through this process that the proper place for a student waiting for his session was in the waiting room, not popping in and out of other rooms. The proper position was in a chair, and the proper condition was feet on the floor, bottom on the seat. Stan moved on to being able to have order as he walked through the center and the halls at school, to organizing his school materials in his backpack, and finally to creating organization on a page.

Understanding order and disorder is a good starting point for exploring behavior and consequences. Students with challenges in the area of executive function are often very unaware of why things happen the way they do. They don't understand why they are the ones that always have to stay in for recess, why other kids are mad at them, or why they never seem to have enough time to complete the projects that are assigned in class.

Telling children like this to behave or think before they act doesn't work if they have no real sense of the cause and effect relationship between their behavior and the consequences. Even telling them why something happened does not mean that they will do anything differently the next time. Through questioning, a therapist or parent can help them discover:

- What they actually did or said,
- What happened as a result,

- What other things they could have said or done, and what the result would have been, and
- What strategy they could use for a different outcome the next time.

Teaching a child to monitor himself

Carson was bright and inquisitive and he heard everything. When conversations or lessons were going on that did not involve him, he often heard them and commented across the room. When working on his own, he often said his answers or thoughts out loud. Carson noticed everything about everybody, so he often asked questions or made comments about things he noticed that had nothing to do with the lesson.

Being observant is a good thing. Voicing every thought out loud is disruptive. We worked with Carson on recognizing and determining when he should be speaking out loud and when he should use his inner voice. We practiced a cue with him of two quiet taps on the desk. When he heard this, he would say to himself, "Should I be talking out loud or using the voice in my head?"

Once Carson could use the cue at the learning center, we asked his teacher at school to use it also. He was to say, with his inner voice, "Should I be talking out loud or should I be using the voice in my head?" whenever he heard the tap. Having Carson question himself was more effective than telling him to be quiet because it helped him to build an awareness of his behavior so that he could begin to self-monitor and take control.

With repeated practice, Carson no longer needed the teacher's cue to recognize when he was talking out loud or interrupting. He was able to catch and correct himself.

Using strategies to teach executive function and study skills

Learning to create and use strategies to monitor and evaluate behavior and attention is literally training executive function. Applying the use of strategies to problem solving of any kind involves:

- Awareness that there *is* a problem
- Identifying exactly what the problem is

- Coming up with possible solutions or strategies
- Evaluating how well each strategy will work and what the outcome will be
- Deciding on the best solution
- Committing to trying it
- Evaluating whether the outcome was what was expected and hoped for
- Modifying the strategy as needed

These are the steps we use to help children develop executive function and study skills. Through dialoguing, modeling, practicing, and evaluating together, children become more and more capable of managing their own behavior, choices, attention, and studies. Below are some specific strategies for helping students get and stay organized, and examples of how to apply training in executive function.

Use an assignment sheet or agenda daily.

Often, teachers write homework assignments on the board for students to copy onto their assignment sheet or agenda. Here is a strategy for getting into the habit of writing homework down. Modify this to fit your child's specific situation.

Have the child talk through and visualize himself getting to (each) class before the bell rings, getting his agenda out of his backpack, looking up at the board, and writing down the assignment. This should be visualized and verbalized to a parent before going to school and before going to bed each night.

When the student has gotten really good at verbalizing this process aloud, he should continue to visualize before school and before going to bed, but using his inner language to talk himself through the process. Parents can facilitate and monitor this by asking, "What do you need to visualize and mentally talk through before you get out of the car for school (or before you go to sleep tonight)?" Continue this until getting assignments written down in the agenda is a consistent habit.

Make sure all materials for homework are in the backpack.

When writing down an assignment in the agenda, the materials, such as a textbook or study guide that are needed for that assignment, should be put in the backpack immediately. If the materials cannot be put in the backpack because they are being used or are in the student's locker, they should be written on the agenda with a box drawn around them.

Before class is over, or when the student gets to her locker after each class, she should put the text or materials needed into her backpack. She should refer to her agenda to be sure of what she needs.

Before the student leaves school, she needs to double-check her agenda and materials. She should determine a specific time when she will do this. It would be best to do this before leaving the (last) class each day.

Visualize and verbalize this process before bed and before school daily in order to develop a habit.

Have a back-up plan that the student can execute.

Help your child find out if there is a Homework Hotline or website he can go to in order to check on homework assignments on the occasion that he forgets to write them down. If these helps are not available, he should have a buddy he can call. However, he should remember that none of these will be as reliable as writing down his homework completely at the beginning of each class.

Have a set homework time.

Many children have a tendency to rush through homework or put off homework they could be doing in order to do other things of greater interest to them. To help avoid this, have a designated homework time. This is a set amount of time that is put on the daily calendar that is specifically designated for homework. The amount of time should be appropriate to the child's age, grade, and teacher expectations. If she needs more time, she can certainly take it, but there should be a designated amount of time set as uninterrupted homework time each day.

A weekly calendar should be created (before Monday each week) that shows all standing appointments and activities and a set homework time for each day. NOTHING should interrupt the homework time. This is a no phone call, no computer/video games, no appointments time.

If the student finishes her homework before the homework time is done, she should begin studying for upcoming tests, work on long-term projects, read a book for school, or read a book for pleasure. The homework time does not stop early.

It is strongly suggested that no video or computer-type games be played before homework time. This is a completely different kind of thinking that is often addictive and hard to break away from, and that is not conducive to the kind of sustained, focused attention needed for homework.

Have a set homework space.

Have a designated homework space, devoid of visual distractors and fully stocked with items needed for homework such as pencils, calculator, etc. Students can easily find interesting things to divert their attention. The fewer distractions and the less often children need to get up from their workspace, the better. Every time they get up to get something they might need, they have an opportunity to talk and distract themselves from the task.

Have a plan for putting homework away and getting it turned in.

When homework is completed, it should be checked off of the agenda and immediately put into the correct section in the binder. When the student finishes an assignment, a parent can ask, "What do you need to do with your completed homework?" The student should talk himself through the process orally saying, "I've finished my math homework, so I put it in the math section of the binder." Once this is a stable procedure, have him mentally talk himself through the process with his inner language.

Remembering to turn in completed assignments can sometimes be a challenge, especially if the teacher does not have an organized routine or if expectations are different in each class. At the beginning of the school year, discuss how homework is collected in each class. The student should visualize and talk through the process of turning in his homework in each class. He should imagine or mentally "hear" the teacher asking for the homework at the beginning of class and visualize himself putting the homework in the designated homework spot.

Use a long-term calendar.

Using a long-term calendar will require parental guidance until the student has done it enough to become independent with it. Long-term assignments need to be broken down into manageable parts, and each part needs to be written on the calendar. This should be done the day the assignment is given.

Students will learn best how to do this if they are guided through questioning. Here are some sample questions:

- What are the logical pieces of the assignment?
- What order do you need to do these parts in?
- How long will each part take?
- If you have three weeks to complete the assignment, what "due date" should we assign to each part?
- Are there parts that you will need help with? (It is important that students begin to do as much independently as possible. Having them help determine which parts they think they will need parent or tutor help with places more value on that time and assistance. It also helps students to see themselves as having more control and being capable).

These organizational strategies are well worth the time and effort that it takes to develop them into habits. If done with great consistency, they will become lifetime habits that support the student throughout his school and adult life.

The value of organization skills

Many students do not automatically acquire organizational skills so they must be taught, practiced, and monitored. If parents and students work together in this process, exploring what works, being flexible and finding new solutions, and developing solid habits, the outcomes will be:

- Greater independence
- Proud parents
- Confident students
- Improved problem solving
- More flexible thinking
- Growth in executive function

When should parents start working on organizational skills with their children? The answer to this is NOW! Skills and strategies will need to be modified to match the age and grade of the child, but even in kindergarten, simple habits can be developed to get materials ready for school the day before and have a specific place to put them. Many schools give homework as early as kindergarten or first grade, so having a set homework time, space, and place to put completed homework is applicable even at a young age. The earlier habits are developed, the easier it will be down the road.

Teaching children executive function skills is teaching them life skills. These are the skills that help children become thinkers and problem solvers. They allow children to reason and approach new learning and unfamiliar situations, with ease instead of fear.

Action items. . .
- Go to www.LearningDisability.com.
  Under "Free Articles," read:
    * "Order . . . The Missing Link for Many."
    * "Conquering Those End of Chapter Questions."
    * "Winning the Homework Battle."

CHAPTER 20

Other Causes of Learning Problems

Helping Children with Autistic Spectrum Disorders,
Various Syndromes, and Brain Injury

In this chapter. . .

- Why you shouldn't give up on children with autism
- How the learning skills continuum can reveal hidden potential
- Why children with brain injuries need cognitive retraining

Improvement is possible in most cases

We've been quite bold in our claims that learning disabilities can be corrected. We can say this because we have seen it so many times over so many years. But what about children with autism, Asperger syndrome, genetic disorders, or other challenges that affect their learning but don't really fit the learning disability-type category? Can the Learning Skills Continuum Approach help them?

While the prognosis may not be quite as secure and easy to predict, the answer is YES! Here's the bottom line: We are teaching children. The Learning Skills Continuum gives us a glimpse into what the brain needs in order to learn. The process still applies. The questions to ask are:

- What is keeping this child from learning or functioning as easily as he could be?
- What do the symptoms look like?
- What are the underlying skills that are not supporting this learner well enough?

With our roadmap in hand, we can begin to develop the supporting skills that students need to be the most independent and functional learners they can be. The labels these children carry with them should be helpful in understanding their learning style and needs, but should never be used to limit them. We really don't know what potential will be uncovered when the brain gets more accurate and complete information to think with.

Surprising results can occur

This week, I received a high school graduation announcement from Wayne, a boy who came to the learning center as an autistic child with all the classic symptoms. His therapy spanned a number of years, at first fairly intensively, and then just a couple of hours a week. When he left us as a high school sophomore, he no longer carried the autistic label.

Is this a once in a lifetime case? No. Is it a sure thing? No. But what we do know is that by working with the Learning Skills Continuum, the quality of a child's and family's life can change; level of function can change.

Mitch had virtually no language and no attention span when he began at the learning center. He was simply not "present" or connected in sessions, at school, or at home. Now, Mitch spontaneously asks short questions and communicates his needs. He moves more easily and can participate with his family and at school in a more normal fashion. He creates stories from pictures with guidance and is happier and more present. Mitch will probably not earn a high school diploma, but the quality of his life is forever changed and will continue to change as his neurodevelopmental and processing skills improve.

Jodie is a high school student in regular classes with some support at school. She has already passed algebra and is on her way to graduating. But it wasn't always this way for her.

Jodie has Fragile X Syndrome, a genetic disorder that can cause learning disabilities, mental retardation, speech and language delays, and autistic behaviors. When her school district sent her to the learning center for sixty hours of treatment, we were told, "Just do whatever you want; she's never going to learn." That sounded like a challenge to me.

Language and learning have been very difficult for Jodie. It hasn't been an easy road or a quick fix, but she has come a long way from the little girl who never looked you in the eye, rarely spoke, couldn't read, couldn't do math, and mostly cried. She is an active high school student with friends and extra-curricular activities. Learning is a challenge, but she's making it in the regular high school curriculum with a limited amount of support. Jodie has a beautiful smile and converses quietly but fairly easily.

This is a far, far cry from a child without the capability to learn. The brain was meant to learn. When we can provide it the information it needs, it can do what it's meant to do.

A word about brain injury

When the brain is injured through a concussion, surgery, or trauma, the effect on learning can be very similar to a learning disability. The person may have trouble accessing, remembering, understanding, or connecting information. In other words, learning/processing skills may be affected.

Because of brain plasticity studies, we know that the brain can change in response to training. Part of the recovery process for brain injury must include cognitive retraining so that the neural connections can be repaired or re-developed. This may involve any or all levels of the learning skills continuum.

The Learning Skills Continuum Approach is not a magic bullet, but it is a clinically proven, science-based, highly successful approach to developing the underlying skills needed for successful learning at any age.

CHAPTER 21

Finding Help

What to do when you're at your wit's end

In this chapter. . .

- The types of professionals who deal with learning disabilities
- Criteria for screening professionals to find the right one for your child
- What to do if you can't find a suitable professional in your area
- Getting assistance from your child's school
- Finding a permanent solution for your child

"What do I do when I'm at my wit's end?"

"I'm at my wit's end. I'm the parent of a child who's struggling in school. I feel like I've tried everything, but it hasn't really gotten better. We still spend hours and hours doing homework. We still have tears and fights. The teacher still says my child isn't trying hard enough. What do I do now?"

We hear stories like this every day. Parents don't want to see their children suffer and they don't want to accept a band-aid approach. They want their smart kids to have a chance at liking school, enjoying reading and learning, and going to college. But they don't know where to turn.

Four kinds of help available

In most communities, there are four kinds of professionals available to offer you services:

1. **Assessment** - Most psychologists (clinical, educational), psychiatrists, neurologists, and pediatricians offer some kind of assessment.

These professionals can often give you a diagnosis or some idea about what's going on with your child, but few of them will actually have services in place to make the needed changes.

2. **Research** – There are private organizations as well as colleges and universities that do research. That means that some of the students they serve get experimental programs while the others don't receive anything special. Good research will not tell the participants which group they are in.

3. **Advocates** – Advocates play a special role in helping students get all the services (school and community) they are entitled to.

4. **Intervention** – These are the people whose main goal is to make *changes* in what students can actually do. The next step after assessment, after we know what is keeping a child from learning as easily as he should, is to do something about it, to build the weak and missing skills needed to make learning easy.

There are many disciplines that offer help. These include: speech therapists, occupational therapists, developmental or behavioral optometrists, educational therapists, learning centers, neurodevelopmentalists, neurofeedback providers, and tutors.

Because the underlying skills that support learning fall on a fairly broad continuum, it is helpful when the professional works across traditional discipline boundaries rather than on a specific, narrow set of skills.

What has been described in this book falls under the category of intervention.

What kind of help should I look for?

I have no doubt you've found your child in the pages of this book. You probably even have an idea where the breakdown is happening on the Learning Skills Continuum. So you have a basic knowledge of where the underlying trouble spots are, what needs to be strengthened, and in what order the issues must be addressed. Now your challenge is to find someone of like mind to work with your child through the process.

As you begin to look for therapists in your area, you can check with learning centers, developmental optometrists, occupational therapists, speech therapists, educational therapists, or others who provide intervention. Look at these people's ads, ask to talk to current or former clients, and interview the specialist.

Throughout this book, we've discussed a concept that may have been totally a dream for you until now: that your son or daughter can permanently overcome the underlying issues that are causing the problem.

Today, the idea of permanent solutions is not widely held among professionals treating children for learning disabilities. Despite the consistent, often miraculous, results that we see in our center, I'm routinely challenged by teachers, school administrators, doctors, and clinicians who insist, "It can't be done."

As in other professional fields, there's never widespread belief that something is possible, until someone actually does it. Then those looking for a better way immediately want to be a part of the breakthrough. A belief or a mindset about what can and can't be done may be the only reason a breakthrough doesn't occur.

Let me give you an example from sports. In 1852, Charles Westhall ran a one-mile race in 4 minutes and 28 seconds. His record was broken many times in the years that followed, but the accepted belief at that time was that no human could run a mile in four minutes.

And yet, in 1954, Roger Bannister broke the four-minute threshold. As impressive as that was, even more stunning was that once people saw it *could* be done, it was inevitable it *would* be done. In fact, less than eight weeks later, John Landy of Australia not only ran a four-minute mile, he beat Bannister's record.

The same principle applies in the treatment of learning disabilities. You know children are enjoying permanent results. Now **you know your child can, too**. Your next step is to find professionals who also know it can be done. You don't want to get stuck in the same rut you've been in, trying to prop up your child or give him even more coping techniques.

Since you're the parent—and now a much better informed parent—here is what you need to know before working with a professional in the field. These are the basic criteria I recommend you use to screen a professional's services before engaging them:

- How do they view learning problems? Do they look at them as permanent and something to learn to compensate for, or are they talking about **solving underlying issues that will permanently correct the problem**?
- How broad is their picture? Are they looking at just one aspect of the learning challenge or can they talk to you about an **overall picture of the underlying issues contributing to the problem**?
- Do they seem to **understand the Learning Skills Continuum** even if they don't use those words?
- Do they appear to have **multiple approaches** or just one approach that is applied to everyone?
- Is the service provided on a **one-to-one basis**?

What if I can't find someone like this in my area?

Finding someone in your area who does this kind of work may be difficult. Through the professional trainings we have taken and provided in this field, we have networked with many professionals who use the techniques we do. Here are some options for you if you can't locate the right kind of help:

1. Contact us through www.FixLearningSkills.com. If we know or have trained someone in your area, we will happily refer you.
2. Call or email us to find out how we can help you provide your child the help he needs through a Distance Learning Program.
3. Do an intensive learning program at the Stowell Learning Center, which will compress many months of therapy into weeks.
4. Complete a short intensive training for parent and child, and then work on a distance learning basis.

Get help from your child's school.

There are services for struggling students at school, and you should take advantage of them if you can. You want people paying attention to your child and you want your child to get all the support she can to keep up and be more comfortable in school.

Just be aware that these are *support* services. They are not generally designed to solve the real problem. You will almost certainly have to get outside help to correct the underlying issues that are causing the learning challenges.

Now you know there's a permanent solution.

It's amazing how many parents come to us, or colleagues we've trained, who are able to tell us in detail exactly the diagnosis (or misdiagnosis) of their child's learning disability. Many have mastered the specific clinical terms, the list of symptoms, including the hidden or lesser-known indicators for a particular problem.

But at some point, what we really want is to make changes in the student's skills. Finding out that a child has a learning disability or is dyslexic can be very helpful in understanding and empathizing with him. But the critical step is to build the skills so that the student's performance no longer reflects that diagnosis.

Now you know that some professionals have broken through the limits. From this moment on, I encourage you to think in terms of a resolution. Even if it doesn't happen overnight, it can happen.

We get excited *every* day with the little changes that students make that take them one step closer to learning easily and independently. Maybe it's noticing and trying to read road signs for the first time. Maybe it's a lonely child making a friend. Perhaps it's a young teen who remembers three days in a row to turn in his homework, or an A on a spelling test, a clearly spoken thought, or going after a difficult task instead of shutting down. These are the moments when children and parents realize that this is *real*. Life really can change.

Trish did not want to spend her summer at the learning center. In fact, her attitude was so bad before she started that her mom was on the verge of giving up the idea altogether. But after her first few weeks of therapy, Trish could feel that she was able to do things without working quite so hard. She didn't feel as lost and confused.

She begged her mom to continue even after her summer program was over, because she knew things were changing. "I don't want to be the bad kid at school anymore. I want to pass the CAHSEE (California High School Exit Exam) and graduate."

There is nothing like success to help students rediscover their potential and desire to learn. That is the gift that targeted learning skills training brings. Small improvements reap huge rewards scholastically, socially, and emotionally.

And that means you will no longer be at wit's end, but at a whole new beginning for you and your child.

RESOURCES

Now that you have a basic understanding of how your child can overcome the challenges of learning disabilities, whether they are mild or severe, you will want additional resources to help you on your journey.

We have a site you've seen mentioned throughout this book, which is specifically for parents. We are adding new articles, audio, and video clips regularly to make this your go-to resource to find answers:

www.FixLearningSkills.com

In addition, we have articles and resources for parents at the Stowell Learning Center site:

www.LearningDisability.com

Training for Professionals and Educators

If the material in this book has struck a chord with you, and you want to be on the leading edge to see breakthrough results with children in your practice, we offer training in the approaches and programs mentioned throughout this book.

For further information, go to:
www.Learning100.com
or call
909-598-9796

Jill Stowell is available for speaking engagements.
Stowell Learning Center
15192 Central Avenue
Chino, CA 91710-7656
909-598-2482

NOTES

Chapter 6

1. A description of Patricia Lindamood's findings regarding an aspect of auditory perception that she termed "auditory conceptual function" can be found on pages 42- 46 of *The A.D.D. Program: Auditory Discrimination in Depth, Book 1: Understanding the Program* by Charles H. and Patricia C. Lindamood. Auditory conceptual function is now called "phonemic awareness" and is considered a key predictor in success or failure in reading.

2. Dr. Michael Merzenich presented his brain plasticity research and findings at the Scientific Learning Conference in Berkeley, CA on March 9, 1998.

   In Chapter 3 entitled <u>Redesigning the Brain</u>, of his book *The Brain That Changes Itself*, Norman Doidge, M.D. describes Dr. Merzenich's journey and discoveries regarding brain plasticity.

3. Doidge, Norman, M.D. *The Brain That Changes Itself: stories of personal triumph from the frontiers of brain science.* New York, NY: Penguin Group, 2007, pages 47-48.

Chapter 9

1. Lyon, G. Reid and Krasnegor, Norman A. *Attention, Memory, and Executive Function.* Baltimore, MD: Paul H. Brookes Publishing Co., 2005, pg. 3.

2. A discussion of interventions and treatments for ADD can be found on pages 211 – 222 of Dr. Daniel Amen's book *Healing ADD: The Breakthrough Program That Allows You to See and Heal the 6 Types of ADD.*

3. Information on when to order a SPECT Study and other questions about this procedure can be found on pages 286 – 309 of Dr. Daniel Amen's book *Healing ADD: The Breakthrough Program That Allows You to See and Heal the 6 Types of ADD.*

Chapter 10

1. *Like Sound Through Water* by Karen Foli is a poignant description of a mother's search for answers to her child's difficult behavior and lack of language. It provides the reader with a profound picture of a severe auditory processing disorder.

2. Tomatis, Alfred, M.D. *The Conscious Ear.* Barrytown, NY: Station Hill Press, 1991, page 186.

Chapter 12

1. Farmer, Jeanette. *Training the Brain to Pay Attention the Write Way.* Denver, CO: WriteBrain Press, 1998, page 1.

2. Levine, Mel, M.D. *A Mind at a Time.* NY: Simon and Schuster, 2002, page 171.

3. Truch, Stephen, Ph.D. *Discover Math*™. Calgary, AB, Canada: The Reading Foundation, 2000.

Chapter 13

1. Perlmutter, David, M.D. *The Better Brain Book.* New York, NY: Riverhead Books, 2004, page 61.

2. Perlmutter, David, M.D.. *The Better Brain Book.* New York, NY: Riverhead Books, 2004, page 62.

3. Duffy, William. *Sugar Blues.* Grand Central Publishing, 1986, page 138.

4. Rapp, Doris, M.D. *Is This Your Child?* New York, NY: William Morrow and Company, Inc., 1991, pages 157, 172.

5. Smith, Joan, Ph.D. *Learning Victories.* Sacramento, CA: Learning Time Products, Inc., 1998, pages 63 - 91.

6. Rapp, Doris, M.D. *Is This Your Child?* New York, NY: William Morrow and Company, Inc., 1991, pages 157-193. This section describes in detail the steps needed to use an elimination diet to determine a child's food sensitivities and allergies.

Chapter 14

1. Samonas Sound Therapy was developed by Ingo Steinbach. Samonas Sound Therapy programs are prescribed and monitored by a certified Samonas Therapist.

2. Auditory Stimulation and Training (AST) uses a combination of Samonas Sound Therapy and directed audio-vocal training lessons to stimulate auditory processing and improve listening, speaking, comprehension, reading, and spelling. There are three specific training programs: AST-Reading and Spelling, AST-Comprehension, and AST-Language. AST programs were developed by Jill Stowell.

3. Core Learning Skills Training is a program of movement and visual skills activities that integrates primitive reflexes, improves body and attention awareness and control, develops visual skills, spatial orientation, and internal timing and organization. It is supported by Samonas Sound Therapy and was compiled by Jill Stowell.

4. PACE, developed by Dr. Ken Gibson, stands for Processing and Cognitive Enhancement. It is a comprehensive processing skills program that is provided to students on a one-to-one basis. It provides cognitive training in memory, attention, auditory and

visual processing, phonemic awareness, processing speed, and logic and reasoning.

Chapter 15

1. Ratey, John J., M.D. *A User's Guide to the Brain*. New York: Vintage Books, 2002, page 148.

2. The HeartMath organization has a number of products that include explanation and use of the heart breathing strategy. These can be found at www.heartmath.com. *Freeze Framer* by Doc Childre, noted in the bibliography, describes the biological foundation for this technique and a number of applications of it.

Chapter 16

1. The Tomatis Listening Test, developed by Alfred Tomatis, M.D., uses a specially calibrated audiometer to evaluate and compare a person's listening skills through air and bone conducted sound. The Tomatis Listening Test is not a hearing test, but a measure that gives insight into an individual's ability to attend, or pay attention to, sound.

Chapter 17

1. We have found these cognitive training programs to be highly successful with students ages 6 or 7 - adult. Each is noted in the bibliography.

Chapter 18

1. The books and programs mentioned for use with attention training are noted in the bibliography. Training in most of the techniques is also available by visiting the authors' websites.

2. The alignment procedure can be found on pages 163-170 of the *Gift of Learning* by Ronald Davis.

3. Chapter four of *The Gift of Dyslexia* by Ronald Davis explains how small, common sight words such as *the, of,* and *if* can be confusing and disorienting for dyslexic readers.

Chapter 19

1. Further information about the concept of order as opposed to disorder is discussed on pages 208–220 of *The Gift of Learning* by Ronald Davis.

2. The concept mastery technique is discussed on pages 200–203 of *The Gift of Learning* by Ronald Davis.

BIBLIOGRAPHY

Amen, Daniel, M.D. *Healing ADD: The Breakthrough Program That Allows You to See and Heal the 6 Types of ADD.* New York, NY: The Berkley Publishing Group, 2001.

Amen, Daniel, M.D. *Making a Good Brain Great.* U.S.: Harmony Books, 2005.

Belgau, Frank and Belgau, Beverly. *Learning Breakthrough Program.* Port Angeles, WA: Balametrics, Inc., 1982, Revised 2001.

Bellis, Teri James, Ph.D. *When the Brain Can't Hear.* New York, NY: Pocket Books, 2002.

Berne, Samuel A., O.D., FCOVD. *Creating Your Personal Vision.* Santa Fe, NM: Color Stone Press, 2005.

Berne, Samuel A., O.D., FCOVD. *Without Ritalin: A Natural Approach to ADD.* Santa Fe, NM: Color Stone Press, 2006.

Berne, Samuel A., OD, FCOVD, FCSO. Seminar: Vision, Learning, and Development. 2006.

Beuret, Lawrence, M.D., S.C. (1995). "NDD Checklist." *Learning 100.* Web. 2009.

Boon, Rosemary. (n.d.). "Neurodevelopmental Therapy: Inhibition of Primitive Reflexes." *Learning Discovery Psychological Services.* Web. 2009.

Brown, Thomas, Ph.D. Attention Deficit Disorder: *The Unfocused Mind in Children and Adults.* New Haven and London: Yale University Press, 2005.

Bibliography

Childre, Doc. *Freeze Framer.* Boulder Creek, CA: Planetary Publications, 1994.

Davis, Ronald with Braun, Eldon. *The Gift of Dyslexia.* New York, NY: Perigree Trade, 1997.

Davis, Ronald with Braun, Eldon. *The Gift of Learning.* New York, NY: The Berkley Publishing Group, 2003.

Dennison, Paul, Ph.D. and Dennison, Gail. *Brain Gym® Teacher's Edition Revised.* Ventura, CA: Edu-Kinesthetics, Inc., 1998.

DeNoon, Daniel J., Reviewed by Chang, Louise, M.D. (2006) "Ritalin for Preschoolers? Study Shows Drug Provides 'Moderate Help' for Preschool Kids with ADHD." *WebMD Health News.* Web. 2009.

Doidge, Norman, M.D. *The Brain That Changes Itself: stories of personal triumph from the frontiers of brain science.* New York, NY: Penguin Group, 2007.

Duffy, William. *Sugar Blues.* Grand Central Publishing, 1986.

Feurstein, Reuven, M.D. *Instrumental Enrichment: An intervention program for cognitive intelligence.* Baltimore, MD: University Park Press, 1985.

Farmer, Jeannette. *Train the Brain to Pay Attention the Write Way.* Denver, CO: WriteBrain Press, 1995.

Foli, Karen. *Like Sound Through Water.* New York, NY: Atria Books, 2003.

Gibson, Ken, D.O. *Processing and Cognitive Enhancement* (PACE). Colorado Springs, CO: Ken Gibson, 2001.

Goddard, Sally. *Reflexes, Learning, and Behavior, a Window into the Child's Mind.* Eugene, OR: Fernridge Press, 2002.

Gold, Svea. *If Kids Just Came with Instruction Sheets*. Eugene, OR: Fernridge Press, 1997.

Hannaford, Carla, Ph.D. *Smart Moves*. Salt Lake City, UT: Great River Books, 1995.

Learning Enhancement Corp. *Brainware Safari*. Chicago, IL: Learning enhancement Corporation, 2005.

Levine, Mel, M.D. *A Mind at a Time*. NY: Simon and Schuster, 2002.

Levine, Mel, M.D. *All Kinds of Minds*. Cambridge, MA: Educator's Publishing Service, 1995.

Lindamood, Charles H. and Lindamood, Patricia C. *The A.D.D. Program: Auditory Discrimination in Depth, Book 1: Understanding the Program*. U.S.A.: DLM Teaching Resources, 1979.

Lyon, G. Reid and Krasnegor, Norman A. *Attention, Memory, and Executive Function*. Baltimore, MD: Paul H. Brookes Publishing Co., 2005.

Moyers, Gayle. *Learning Ears*. Austin, TX: Moyers Learning Systems 2006.

Perlmutter, David, M.D. *The Better Brain Book*. New York, NY: Riverhead Books, 2004.

Pohlman, Craig, Ph.D. (May 15, 2008). "Neurodevelopmental Take on Executive Functions." *Learning Landscape: All Kinds of Minds*. Web. 2009.

Prelutsky, Jack and Smith, Lane. *Hooray for Diffendoofer Day*. New York: Alfred A. Knopf, Inc. 1998.

Rapp, Doris, M.D. *Is This Your Child?* New York, NY: William Morrow and Company, Inc., 1991.

Bibliography

Ratey, John, M.D. *A User's Guide to the Brain: Perception, Attention, and the Four Theaters of the Brain.* NY: Random House, 2002.

Sollier, Pierre. *Listening for Wellness.* Walnut Creek, CA: The Mozart Center Press, 2005.

Smith, Joan, Ph.D. *Learning Victories.* Sacramento, CA: Learning Time Products, Inc., 1998.

Smith, Joan, Ph.D. *You Don't Have to Be Dyslexic.* Sacramento, CA: Learning Time Products, Inc., 1996.

Smith, Joan, Ph.D. Training Courses: Dyslexia Remediation Specialist Certification and EDU-Therapeutics Trainer Certification, 1999, 2002.

Steinbach, Ingo. *Samonas Sound Therapy.* Keelinghusen, Germany: Techau Verlog, 1997.

Stephey, Douglas. *Brain Spark.* Covina, CA: Douglas Stephey, 2008.

Sunbeck, Deborah, Ph.D. *The Complete Infinity Walk, Book I: The Physical Self.* USA: The Leonardo Foundation Press, 2002.

Sutton, Albert, O.D. *Building a Visual Space World, Volumes 1 and 2.* Santa Ana, CA: Optometric Extension Program Foundation, 1985.

Tomatis, Alfred, M.D. *The Conscious Ear.* Barrytown, NY: Station Hill Press, 1991.

Tomatis, Alfred, M.D. *The Ear and the Voice.* Lanham, MD: Scarecrow Press, 1997.

Truch, Stephen, Ph.D. *Discover Math*™. Calgary, AB, Canada: The Reading Foundation, 2000.

About the Author: Jill Stowell, M.S. is the founder and director of Stowell Learning Centers, Inc. serving children and adults with various learning and attention challenges. She holds a masters degree in education, California teaching credentials in regular education and learning handicaps, and is a certified Dyslexia Remediation Specialist. Jill is the author of several learning skills development programs and teaches professional seminars for educators who want to further the mission of eliminating learning disabilities.

Made in the USA
San Bernardino, CA
06 February 2013